THE CASE OF THE

Spurious Spinster

Erle Stanley Gardner

THE CASE OF THE
Spurious Spinster

WALTER J. BLACK · ROSLYN, N. Y.

THE CASE OF THE

Spurious Spinster

Chapter One

Sue Fisher had to sign the register in the office-building elevator because it was Saturday morning and all of the offices were closed.

Sue had been looking forward to a restful weekend but a wire announcing that Amelia Corning was due to arrive from South America on Monday morning necessitated a lot of last-minute statements and reports which she had been unable to get together by quitting time Friday night. So she had promised Endicott Campbell, manager of the Corning Mining, Smelting & Investment Company, that she would come in Saturday morning, finish typing the reports and have everything on his desk so that the statements would be available the first thing Monday morning.

The situation was further complicated by the fact that in addition to an arthritic condition which confined her to a wheel chair, Amelia Corning was rapidly losing her eyesight. In fact, there were rumors from South America that she had already lost her vision to such an extent that she could only tell the difference between light and dark, and people were hazy, blurred figures whose features were indistinguishable.

Susan Fisher had been with the firm for more than a year and knew Amelia Corning only by her stiff, cramped signature which from time to time appeared at the bottom of irascible letters of brief instructions.

By ten thirty, when Sue Fisher was well immersed in her work, she heard the patter of running feet, then the sound of knuckles on the door and a childish treble saying, "Oh, Miss Sue, Miss Sue."

For a moment, Sue Fisher's face softened. Then she frowned with annoyance. Carleton Campbell, the boss's seven-year-old son, worshipped the ground she walked on and Sue, in turn, was strangely drawn to the youngster. But Elizabeth Dow, the governess, was, Sue

3

felt, more and more inclined to wish off some of her responsibilities and disciplinary problems on Sue's shoulders.

Sue shut off the motor on the electric typewriter, crossed her secretarial office, entered the reception room and opened the door.

Carleton Campbell, his eyes shining with eagerness, held up a shoe box for her inspection.

"Hello, Miss Sue. Hello, Miss Sue," he said.

Elizabeth Dow, moving steadily and deliberately on her low-heeled heavy walking shoes, came marching down the corridor.

Sue put her arm around the boy, lifted him up, kissed him, then stood waiting for Elizabeth Dow, who very typically refrained from quickening her pace in the slightest, nor would she deign to exchange a greeting until she was close enough so there was no necessity of raising her voice in the slightest.

"Good morning, Susan," she said, formally.

"Good morning, Elizabeth."

"I dropped in because they told me you were going to be here this morning."

"Yes," Sue said. "I have work to do." And then, after a properly impressive pause, added, "A very important job. We're working against a deadline."

"I see," Elizabeth Dow said, her voice showing her utter indifference to the urgency of the matter. Elizabeth Dow was affected only by problems which were important to Elizabeth Dow. Other persons' problems made not the slightest difference to her.

"Sue," she said, "would you be a dear and watch Carleton for thirty minutes? I have a very important personal appointment and I just can't take him with me . . . and you know you're the only one he'll stay with."

Sue glanced at her wrist watch. She knew the thirty minutes could be at least forty-five and might well be an hour.

"Well . . ." She hesitated and again looked at the watch.

"I wouldn't ask it of you for myself," Elizabeth Dow said, "but Carleton has some things he wants to talk over with you and he's been rather upset this morning. I know if I left him with the housekeeper in his present state he'd be a nervous wreck by the time I got back, and she would, too."

"Oh, please, Miss Sue," Carleton pleaded. "Let me stay here with you. I want to talk."

"All right," Susan said, "but you're going to have to be a good boy, Carleton. You're going to have to sit in a chair and watch Sue work. I have some very important statements to get out."

"I'll be good," Carleton promised, climbing into a chair and seating himself with his hands folded on the shoe box.

Elizabeth Dow, apparently fearful that something would happen to change Sue's mind, headed for the door. "It will be only a few minutes," she promised, and was gone.

Sue smiled at Carleton. "What's in the box?" she asked.

"Treasure," he said.

Sue regarded the box with sudden apprehension. "Now look here, Carleton," she said, "you haven't any toads or anything alive in that box?"

He smiled and shook his head. "This isn't my treasure box," he said, "it's Daddy's."

"What do you mean?"

"Daddy keeps his treasure box upstairs. Last night he let me put my treasure in his closet. He said he'd trade treasures with me any time I wanted. So this morning I took *his* treasure."

The words poured out with Carleton's childish accent and were spoken so rapidly that one word seemed literally to tread on the heels of another as they left the child's lips.

Susan regarded the box thoughtfully. "Did I understand you right, Carleton?" she asked. "This is Daddy's treasure?"

"It's my treasure now," Carleton said. "Daddy said we could trade treasures but he'd want his back and he'd give me mine back."

"What about *your* treasure box? What kind of a box was it?"

"Just like this," Carleton said. "Daddy doesn't buy shoes in stores. Daddy buys shoes by mail. When they come, my daddy takes the shoes out of the boxes and puts the shoes in the closet."

"Yes, I know," Susan said, smiling. "I make out the orders for his shoes. He has a particular brand of shoes that he likes and he has rather an odd size. Does your daddy know that you have his treasure box?"

"He said we could trade," Carleton said.

"When?"

"Oh, a while back."

"I thought your daddy was going to go out on the golf course this morning."

"He said we could trade," Carleton repeated.

Susan said, "I'd better look in your daddy's treasure box, Carleton, just to see."

He made a convulsive grasping gesture, pressing the box into his stomach and bending over. "No!" he screamed. "That was the trouble with Miss Dow."

"How did that make trouble, Carleton?"

"She wanted to take it away."

"Why?"

"I don't know."

"I'm not talking about taking it away," Susan said. "I just thought we ought to look in it. Don't you think we should?"

He said nothing, but clung to the box.

"You don't know what's in it, do you?"

"Treasure," he said.

"What was in *your* treasure box, Carleton?"

"Lots of things."

"I wonder if your daddy has as many treasures as you do. Do you think he does?"

"I don't know."

"Wouldn't it be fun to find out?" she said, her voice containing an invitation to adventure.

"It's tied up," Carleton said.

Susan smiled at him. "I'm awfully good at knots," she said, and then frowned thoughtfully. "Perhaps, though, those knots would be too much for us. Let's take a look at them, just to see."

Carleton let her inspect the twine around the box.

As soon as she saw the neat square knot she knew that this had not been tied by childish fingers. Whether or not his explanation of the exchange of treasure boxes was correct, there seemed to be no doubt that this was an adult treasure box.

"Let's see how heavy," she said.

He hesitated for a moment, then let her take the box. She moved it up and down in her two hands, estimating the weight, then handed it back to him. "My," she said, "that's heavy."

He nodded.

The fact that she had returned the box to him without trying to open it did much to reassure him.

"I wonder what makes it so heavy," Susan said. And then added,

"If your daddy has business papers in there, Carleton, we'd have to keep them from getting lost."

He nodded gravely, hanging on to the box. "I won't lose it."

"Do you know the difference between a square knot and a granny knot?" Susan asked.

"My granny is dead," he said.

"No, no, not your grandmother, but the knot they call the granny. Look, this is tied with a square knot. See? Here, let me show you."

Having engaged his attention with the box still on the child's lap, Susan worked away at the knot until it was untied. "See how easy it is to untie that kind of a knot?" she said. "Now, a granny is the name of another knot. It's the kind of a knot you would be very apt to tie if you didn't know knots."

Pretending to show Carleton the different methods of tying the string, Susan managed to get the knotted fish twine off the box. She left the box in Carleton's lap but surreptitiously raised a corner of the cover as she got to her knees in order to readjust the string.

What Susan saw stopped her cold. The box was well filled with green currency and the bills Susan saw in that first peek into the box were in amounts of one hundred dollars.

Carleton seemed concerned that someone was going to try to take the box from him.

"Does Miss Dow know this is your daddy's treasure box?" Sue asked.

"Of course. She tried to take that box. She wants my treasure. I don't like her. She's bad."

"She was just trying to help," Sue said. "She probably thought that your daddy didn't want you to take his treasure."

"Daddy said we could trade."

"I wonder," Sue said thoughtfully, "if *your* treasure is safe with your daddy. Do you suppose he might lose it?"

The boy's face clouded with the idea.

"I think," Sue said, "that we should find your daddy and tell him that if he takes your treasure he has to be very careful. Perhaps we could give him his back and take yours, and then yours wouldn't get lost. A golf course is a very big place."

"I don't know where my daddy is. He went out in a car."

"I think he was going to play golf this morning," Sue said. "You don't want to lose your treasure, do you?"

"I'm going to keep Daddy's treasure," the child said, his hands gripping the box tightly.

Sue let her face light up with the inspiration of a sudden idea. "Wouldn't it be fine," she said, "to open the safe, the *big* safe, and put the treasure box in there?"

Carleton seemed dubious.

"Then we'd close the safe," Sue said, lowering her voice to a conspiratorial tone, "and Miss Dow couldn't get in there. Nobody could get in. We'd lock it up and the treasure would be safe, and then we could get it again whenever we wanted it."

Carleton's eyes lit up. "Okay," he said in almost an eager whisper, "let's open the safe."

Sue crossed over to the big safe, twisted the dials on the two combinations and finally flung the doors open. She unlocked the inner steel door and then rearranged some papers so as to make room for the box.

"All right," she whispered, "let's hurry. We'll put it in there before Miss Dow gets back."

Carleton was dancing with excitement. "We'll close it and we won't tell her where it is."

"Oh, we can tell her *where* it is," Sue said, "but it won't do her any good. She can't get the safe open. Nobody except your daddy and I can get this safe open."

"Gee, that's swell," Carleton said.

Sue reached for the box. For a moment Carleton hesitated at parting company with it. But then he shoved it into her hands.

"Now we'll get it fitted right in this compartment here," Sue said.

She turned for a moment so that her body hid the box from Carleton, and during that moment lifted the cover.

There were literally thousands of dollars in that box—hundred-dollar bills which had been stacked neatly and snapped with rubber bands. Evidently, Sue thought in her hurried survey, in lots of five thousand dollars each.

Sue fumbled around getting the cover back on the box, said, "We'll have to tie this string again," and carefully tied the fish cord around the box, knotting it in a square knot as she had found it and then pushing the box into the safe.

She hurriedly closed the inner door, twisted the key, then closed the heavy outer doors, pulled the nickeled levers which shot the bolts into place and spun the combinations.

"Now," she said triumphantly, "we've got it where nobody can get it away from you."

Carleton was enthusiastic with childish excitement. "We won't even tell her where it is."

"Oh, if she asks I think we'd better tell her," Sue said. "But . . . you know, we have to keep an attitude of proper respect for Miss Dow, Carleton. She's trying to help you."

"She's mean," Carleton said, pushing out his lips in a pout. "She doesn't like me."

"Oh, yes, she likes you. She likes you a lot," Sue said. "But, you know, she has work to do and she has to make you do things that you don't like to do sometimes. But they're the things that are good for you."

Sue let her face become suddenly thoughtful. "You know," she said, "I think we ought to try and find your daddy and see if he took your treasure box."

"I don't know where daddy went," Carleton said.

"I'll tell you what we'll do," Susan said. "We'll ring up the country club. I think we can find him there. I know he was intending to play golf this morning and he's out on the links someplace."

"Can we put my treasure in the safe, too?" Carleton asked.

"I think so. I think your daddy will let us. Let's see if we can find him."

"He's coming home tonight."

"I know," Sue said, "but he's playing golf and you know he can't carry a box with him while he's playing golf. If he traded treasures, he's probably left your box in the car or somewhere and you wouldn't want anything to happen to your treasure, would you?"

"No."

"Well, let's try and find him."

Sue connected up the switchboard and put through a call to the country club.

"Is Mr. Endicott Campbell on the links?" she asked.

"I'll have to connect you with the office of the pro," the operator said. "Just a moment."

After a few moments, a masculine voice said gruffly, "Golf shop."

"Is Mr. Endicott Campbell on the links this morning?" Sue asked.

"I'd like to speak with him, and it's quite important. This is his office calling and if you—"

"But he isn't here," the voice interrupted.

"Not there?" Sue asked, disappointment in her voice.

"That's right ma'am, he isn't here. Hasn't been here all morning. There was a reservation for him as a member of a foursome, but they canceled out. . . . Sorry."

"Thank you," Sue said, and hung up the telephone.

For a long moment she sat thinking while Carleton watched her, his eyes wide with childish curiosity.

Then abruptly the switchboard buzzed with an incoming call and a red light flashed on the trunk line.

Sue hesitated a moment, then almost automatically plugged in the line. "Corning Mining, Smelting and Investment Company," she said.

A woman's voice, sharply strident, said, "Why isn't anyone here to meet me?"

"I'm sorry," Sue said in her most dulcet voice. "Can you tell me who you are and where you are and—?"

"This is Amelia Corning. I'm at the airport."

"What!" Sue exclaimed.

"Didn't you hear me?"

"I . . . yes . . . why . . . We weren't expecting you until Monday, Miss Corning."

"Monday my foot!" the voice snapped. "I sent you a wire. You should have met me. This is an imposition. I had to get someone to wheel me up to a phone booth and dial the phone for me. Now, you get out here! Who are you? Who's talking?"

"This is Susan Fisher, the confidential secretary of Mr. Endicott Campbell," Sue said.

"Where's Mr. Campbell?"

"He isn't here this morning. This is Saturday morning, you know."

"I know what day it is. Don't tell me what day it is!" the woman snapped. "All right, get out here. I'll wait. I've had a lot of problems with baggage and all the rest of it and I'm tired."

The receiver was slammed at the other end of the line.

Susan hung up in a daze, turned to Carleton, said, "Carleton, do you know where Miss Dow was going?"

"I think to the bank," Carleton said.

"To the bank!" Susan exclaimed.

"I think the bank."

"On Saturday morning?" Sue said. "The banks aren't open on Saturday . . . oh, wait a minute. There's one branch that is open."

She picked up the telephone book and was looking up the number of the bank when she heard the sound of steady, deliberate steps in the corridor outside; then the door to the entrance room opened and Elizabeth Dow stood on the threshold. "Was he much trouble?" she asked.

"He's a dear," Sue said. "Just a darling. But I've got to run—and I've simply got to find Mr. Campbell. Do you know where he is?"

"Playing golf, I think. You better try the country club—that is, if it's *really* important. I don't think he'd want to be disturbed—"

"I'll be the judge of that," Sue interrupted somewhat shortly. "I've tried the country club. I can't locate him there. I simply have to know *where* he is."

The governess shook her head.

"Do you know the names of the people he was going to be playing with?"

Again she shook her head.

"Well, I haven't time to mess with it now," Sue said. "Come on, I'm closing up the office. Let's go."

"Where are you going?" the governess asked.

"I have a business matter to attend to, a very important business matter. It's an emergency. If you see Mr. Campbell, tell him that he must get in touch with me at once. At once, do you understand? It's a major emergency."

Elizabeth Dow looked at her curiously. "I think I should know more than that if I'm to give him a message that will make any sense to him."

"Tell him to get in touch with me immediately on a matter of the greatest importance. Tell him it's a major emergency," Sue said. "Come on now, let's get out of here."

Elizabeth Dow didn't wish to be hurried. She collected Carleton in a leisurely manner and said, "Where's your box, Carleton?"

Carleton started to say something, then checked himself and looked at Susan Fisher. "We've hid it," he said.

Miss Dow said, "I don't think you should be hiding things like that. We'll need to keep your treasure with us. Where is it?"

"It's safe for the time being," Sue said. "I'll get it later."

Sue all but pushed the governess out of the door. She pulled the door closed, bent down to give Carleton a hug, then literally flew down the corridor to the elevator and rang the bell.

"The box," Miss Dow called after her. "He'll want it and—"

The cage slid smoothly up to the floor. The operator smiled and said, "All finished, Miss Fisher?"

Sue could hear Miss Dow's steps around the bend in the corridor, prayed that the attendant would not hear them. "Yes," she said, "and I've got to get a cab in a hurry."

"All right," the attendant said, "let's go." The door slid shut just as Elizabeth Dow, holding Carleton Campbell firmly by the hand, rounded the bend in the corridor. The assistant janitor who was operating the elevator didn't see them, but for a swift moment Elizabeth Dow's eyes locked with those of Sue Fisher. And, as the door started to close, an expression of angry indignation flooded the face of the governess; then Sue saw only the lights marking the floor numbers as the elevator descended.

She hurried across the lobby and found a taxi at the cab stand near the corner. She jumped into it and said, "I've got to get to the airport. Please get me there as quickly as possible."

After she had started, Sue looked in her purse, wondering if she would have enough money to pay the cab.

It was, she decided, going to be touch and go. She pulled out four one-dollar bills and then removed keys, lipstick and compact so that she could count out the silver change in her purse.

Having decided she could just about make it, she settled back against the cushions, closed her eyes and tried her best to get the situation clarified.

Miss Corning was an irascible but exceedingly clever business-woman. If she could be stalled off until Endicott Campbell could be located, she would ask her questions of the manager. But Sue had a sinking feeling that Amelia Corning was going to ask questions of her; questions that it might be very difficult indeed to answer. In fact, Sue had been asking herself questions during the last few days while they had been getting statements ready in anticipation of Miss Corning's arrival.

There was, for instance, the question of the Mojave mine known as the Mojave Monarch. The company books certainly showed the

Mojave Monarch was operating on a twenty-four-hour basis, three eight-hour shifts a day. But a week ago Sunday, when Susan had taken a drive out by Mojave, she had seen an old weather-beaten sign on a dirt road which said simply: MOJAVE MONARCH. Sue had followed this road out to a place where unpainted buildings were sprawled in the sunlight on the side of a mountain.

Not only did the buildings seem unoccupied, but they had about them an unmistakable aura of abandonment: the peculiar atmosphere which surrounds buildings in the desert that have not known human occupancy for some time. Only the manager's cabin seemed occupied, but no one had answered her knock.

Puzzled, Sue had driven back to Mojave and asked at a service station about the Mojave Monarch. The man she had asked had no personal information, but had relayed the question on to a grizzled miner who had driven up to the station.

The miner had told her there was only one Monarch Mine in the vicinity as far as he knew, and that hadn't been worked for more than two years.

At the time, Susan had felt certain there was some mistake, that there must be a Monarch Mine the old miner didn't know about, and the mine she had found was simply another mine bearing the same name. After all, Monarch was a name which could easily be duplicated simply through coincidence.

During the past week, Sue had taken occasion to consult the records on the Monarch Mine. There was an office in Mojave where the business affairs were administered. The Corning Mining, Smelting & Investment Company simply made regular checks covering expenses.

There were reports from the mine in the files. These reports indicated that engineers felt they were due to break into a big body of high-grade ore. The technical terms meant little or nothing to Sue Fisher when she had given them a hasty perusal. She barely knew the difference between a hanging wall and a foot wall. She did know that the main vein had "faulted out" and at the time the fault had been encountered, the vein was fabulously rich and getting wider.

Sue knew that there had been something in Amelia Corning's correspondence about the Mojave Monarch records. Geological reports had been forwarded to her in South America. That, however, was only one of several matters that had caused Amelia Corning, after a five-year absence from the country, to return to make a personal check on the affairs of the company.

Sue dreaded the barrage of questions which might be asked. She decided to refer everything to Mr. Campbell and play it just as dumb as she knew how.

At the airport Sue paid off the cab. It took every cent she had in her purse to pay the driver and leave him a thirty-five-cent tip.

"I'm sorry about the tip," she apologized. "I had an emergency matter and . . . this is every cent I've got."

"Forget it, lady," the cab driver said with a smile, handing her back the thirty-five cents. "Here, I'll bet you've got some telephoning to do and . . . you take it."

She looked at his rugged face, the kindly smiling eyes and abruptly gave him her hand. "Oh, thank you," she said. "I feel so—so cheap. Actually, I can put this on an expense account, but . . . well, I don't have the cash money with me, that's all."

"Forget it," he told her. "It's a pleasure to carry a lady like you."

Then he was gone and Sue was hurrying toward the waiting room, searching for Amelia Corning, fearful lest she shouldn't find her yet dreading the encounter.

Susan saw Amelia Corning as soon as she entered the waiting room at the airport. It would, in fact, have been impossible to miss her. She sat in a collapsible wheel chair facing the door. Two suitcases and a bag were parked beside the wheel chair. The bags were generously plastered with labels of various South American hotels and resorts. The face was far from prepossessing, being set in grim lines with a long bony chin, a firm, straight nose, high cheekbones and glasses with huge dark-blue lenses which completely concealed the eyes.

Susan approached the figure in the chair.

The woman sat completely motionless. If she saw Susan Fisher approaching, she gave no sign.

"Miss Corning?" Susan asked, trying to keep a quaver out of her voice.

The bony face slowly tilted upward. Susan had the feeling that back of the heavy dark glasses, weak eyes were trying to appraise her. "Yes."

"I'm Susan Fisher, Mr. Campbell's secretary, the one you talked with over the phone when I was in the office."

Susan expected some criticism and was surprised when the woman said, in a voice which had suddenly lost its truculence, "You're a dear, Susan, to get out here so soon."

"I came as soon as I could."

"I know you did. Of course, it seemed like a long time to me waiting here, but I realize you had a long way to travel and you must have started at once. Thank you."

Susan said, "You're—you're very welcome. Now, do we take a cab?"

"Of course we take a cab."

"I'll have to carry your baggage out and—"

"Call the porter."

"Yes, Miss Corning. I—I'm sorry, I—"

"Well, what is it?" the woman snapped, suddenly losing her gracious manner. "I hate people who stumble around and try to put a sugar coating on bad news. What's the trouble?"

"I haven't a cent," Sue said. "I used up all of my meager store of pocket money paying the cab fare out here."

"Don't you have a petty-cash fund at the office available for emergencies? Why isn't there a fund available to trusted employees?"

"I—I don't know. There just isn't."

"There's a safe?"

"Yes . . . of course."

"You have the combination to it?"

"Yes."

"Who else has the combination?"

"Mr. Campbell and the bookkeeper."

"There should be a fund of several hundred dollars kept available for emergency trips. How do you know when I might call on you to take a plane at once for South America?"

Sue Fisher stood in something of a quandary, hardly knowing how to reply to that.

"When you get hold of Mr. Campbell, see that such a fund is available. I may want you to come to South America. You're a good girl, Susan. You're frightened to death. After you get to know me better you won't be so frightened, but you will learn to respect my judgment, you will carry out my orders unhesitatingly. Do you understand? Unhesitatingly."

"Yes, Miss Corning."

"Very well," she said, opening her bag, taking out a billfold and extracting five bills.

"My eyes aren't good. I can't see well in this light. I never know how much money I have with me, but I make it a point to have enough. Here, my dear, are five ten-dollar bills. Charge yourself with fifty dollars expense money."

Susan Fisher said in an odd voice, "Miss Corning, those aren't ten-dollar bills, they're hundred-dollar bills."

"Thank you. I try to keep the hundreds in one side and the tens in the other. I guess my billfold must have got turned around."

Her bony fingers moved to the other side of the thick sheaf of bills, counted out five bills.

"These are tens, Sue?"

"Yes, ma'am."

"All right, that's fifty dollars. That's expense money. Deduct what you paid for the taxicab and now get me a porter and a cab and we'll get started. You have reservations for me?"

"The reservations were for Monday, but . . . we can probably get in."

"My wire wasn't received?"

"No, ma'am."

"It should have been."

"It's probably on the way someplace."

"On the way nothing! I left earlier than I intended to on the spur of the moment. That no-good attendant at the airport to whom I gave a big bill so he could pay for the wire tore up the telegram, put the money in his pocket and went out and got drunk. That's the way with the world these days. No responsibility, no moral stamina, no real downright honesty. All right, Susan, we'll go to the hotel."

Susan secured a porter, a cab, and found herself answering intimate searching questions about the business of the Corning Mining, Smelting & Investment Company during the ride in the taxicab.

At one point, Susan ventured to say, "I do wish you'd save these questions to ask of Mr. Campbell, Miss Corning."

"You're in my employ, aren't you?"

"Yes. But I'm directly under Mr. Campbell."

"I don't care whom you're directly under, you're in *my* employ. You're working for *me*. You're drawing wages that come out of *my* pocket. I want loyalty, I want efficiency and I want co-operation. You'll answer my questions, my child, and we won't have any more of this 'Ask Mr. Campbell' stuff.

"I'm going to the hotel just long enough to check in and get my bags put in my room, then we're going up to the office and you're going to put in the rest of the day answering questions."

"I am?" Sue exclaimed, despair in her voice.

"Yes, my child, *you* are. And you're going to answer them right. I don't want any attempt to shield anyone, you understand. Yourself or anyone else."

"Yes, Miss Corning."

"Now, for your information," she said, "the reason I arrived on Saturday morning instead of Monday is that I knew good and well Endicott Campbell would be out playing golf or doing something of that sort, and I wanted to descend on the office and get some records before he was expecting me. I gave a wire to an attendant but I felt sure he wouldn't send it. You said that you had the combination to the safe. We're going to open it and we're going to take a look. It's going to be a strain on my eyes and I'll have to use a big reading glass, but I'm going to check some of the figures and you're going to give me the information I want.

"Now then, I'm going to ask you a straight question. Have you any reason to believe that Endicott Campbell is dishonest?"

"I . . . why, no."

"Don't talk to me like that."

"Like what?"

"You hesitated after you started to answer the question. I don't want hesitation, I want straightforward answers. Have you any reason to believe Endicott Campbell is dishonest?"

"I don't know."

"Certainly. You don't know that he's dishonest, but do you have any reason to believe that he *may* be dishonest? Yes or no."

"Well," Susan said, "there's one matter that's been bothering me— the Mojave Monarch."

"And that's been bothering *me*. I think we're going to get along together pretty well, Susan, once you've learned to answer questions promptly, frankly and honestly."

At Miss Corning's insistence Susan not only went to the hotel with her but also signed Miss Corning's name on the hotel register for her, then went up to the suite of rooms which had been reserved for Monday, the fifth, yet which the clerk said was presently available and which he had been able to assign for immediate occupancy.

Then, after the briefest of intervals, Sue escorted Miss Corning to the office.

"Now then, my child," Miss Corning said, "I want to see the vouchers in the Mojave Monarch Mine. As you probably know, I instructed Mr. Campbell to have everything ready for me."

Sue said, "The books are in the safe, but all the detailed information seems to be in Mojave."

"All right, the books show generally the expenses of the mine. What has been received from it by way of returns from ore shipments?"

"I can't find those records. I think they are in Mojave. There are reports showing the main vein faulted out, but I know from oral reports Mr. Campbell has made to me there has been quite a quantity of milling ore brought out of the ground."

"What was done with it?"

"I don't know."

"Open up the safe. Let's see what the books show."

Susan opened the safe, unlocked the inner steel door, and pulled out the books pertaining to the Mojave Monarch Gold Mining & Exploration Company.

Miss Corning sent her wheel chair up to within a few inches of the safe, leaned forward to peer from behind those dark glasses. "What's this?" she asked, pointing a long bony finger toward the shoe box which Susan had taken from Carleton Campbell.

For a moment Sue was embarrassed. "Why that . . ." she said, "that's . . . something private, something of my own that I've put in the safe for a few hours because I didn't want to take it with me when I went to the airport and—"

"What is it?" Miss Corning insisted.

"Something personal."

"Love letters?"

"Not exactly."

"All right, what is it? It's in the company safe. You shouldn't be putting your private things in here."

"I wouldn't have put it in there, Miss Corning, if it hadn't been for the fact that you telephoned and your telephone call upset my entire schedule. After all, you know, I'm not supposed to be working today. This is something of a purely private nature."

Miss Corning tilted her head so that the big opaque lenses of her dark glasses were turned directly toward Sue. Then she said, "Humph," and spun the chair around and sent it speeding across the office to the desk where Sue had spread out the books and the statements.

Sue was beginning to hold this woman in awe. Miss Corning had an uncanny ability to read her mind, to interpret the faintest nuance of voice. Her long, big-jointed fingers could wrap around the wheels of the chair and send the vehicle darting about with dazzling speed.

"Now, my dear, my eyes aren't what they should be. I can only read with this big reading glass and it tires my eyes. I'm going to have to rely on you. Where's the sheet showing the summary of expenses?"

Susan got it for her.

"Read me the figures," Miss Corning said.

Sue read off the figures slowly, impressively.

The woman frowned and shook her head. "Don't dawdle along so much. Read them right out. I'll remember them. Just get them out."

Sue read the figures.

When she had finished, Miss Corning cross-examined her on them, recalling figure after figure accurately down to the last penny, as though she had the balance sheet right in front of her.

Then suddenly she had changed the subject. "What about this Oklahoma Royal property?" she asked.

Sue went over to the safe and brought out a statement. At Miss Corning's insistence she read that statement also.

Abruptly Miss Corning said, "I think Endicott Campbell is a crook."

Sue was shocked into frozen silence.

"Get me a suitcase," Miss Corning commanded. "I'm going to take all those papers with me. I want a handwriting expert to look over those. I think most of those checks are phonies. I think they've all been endorsed by Endicott Campbell."

"Why, Miss Corning!" Sue exclaimed. "That—that would be—"

"Exactly," Miss Corning snapped as Sue finished. "That would be

forgery or embezzlement, or both. Now then, I want something that
will hold those records. I want a suitcase—two strong suitcases.
Here . . ."

Miss Corning again picked up her bag, opened it, pulled out the
billfold, extracted two one-hundred-dollar bills, said, "You'll find a
luggage store open around here someplace, probably not a good one
but you'll find one that sells baggage. Those places seem to stay open
somehow at ungodly hours. Go down and get me two very strong
suitcases. I don't want them fancy, I want them strong. Get back here
just as fast as you can."

"Yes, ma'am," Sue said.

"Hurry along now. I know a handwriting expert here in the city
who will go into these things for me. I'm not satisfied with the way
things have been going and you're not either."

"Why, what do you mean?"

"You know good and well what I mean. You're down here working on your Saturday trying to get things straightened up. You've
been wondering what you were going to say to me when I showed
up. You were hoping you wouldn't have to answer any questions,
that Endicott Campbell would be the one to do it."

"I—I—I don't think I should discuss Mr. Campbell with you,
Miss Corning. After all, I work for—"

"Shut up that magpie chatter," the woman snapped, "and go down
and get me those suitcases! I want to get started on this. I want to
have this thing all at my fingertips by Monday morning and I want to
know how to approach Endicott Campbell. I'm not going to lay myself wide open to a lawsuit by accusing him of anything I can't
prove. If I make an accusation I want to be able to prove it. The
way things look now I am going to make an accusation and I want
the facts to back it up. Now, get started."

"Yes ma'am," Sue said, feeling very small and insignificant and
at the same time very much alarmed.

She went down in the elevator and after a couple of fruitless at-
tempts to find a luggage store open on a Saturday afternoon, enlisted
the aid of a cab driver who took her to a rather small but well-
stocked store, waited while she hurriedly selected two strong suitcases, and then drove her back to the office.

Sue, carrying the empty suitcases, found Miss Corning in her wheel chair by the window holding some canceled checks up to the bright afternoon light. A thick-lensed reading glass was held above the checks.

Miss Corning looked up as Sue entered and said, "Humph, just as I thought. This whole deal is completely phoney. You got the suitcases, child?"

"Yes."

"Put them out on that table. Start putting these checks in them. Now, I want that book and all of these statements. I'm going over them in the hotel tonight.

"Now then, just where *is* Endicott Campbell? I mean, where is he supposed to be?"

"I don't know. I called the golf club this morning trying to locate him. He was part of a foursome that had a reservation there but it had been canceled out."

"I want to see him," Miss Corning said, "and I want to see him tonight, at my hotel. Now don't let him come up *here*. I don't want to see him *now,* I don't want to see him at *his* convenience, I want to see him at *mine!* Get on the telephone and get him located."

"I'll have to go to the switchboard," Sue said, "and—"

"I don't care where you have to go," Miss Corning snapped, throwing a bundle of canceled checks into one of the suitcases. "Get on the telephone and get him located. Ring up his golf club. If he isn't there, find out the names of the people who were in the foursome. Ring each one of them up. Get Campbell located. What about his house . . . he wouldn't be there?"

"I don't know. I just don't know where he is, Miss Corning."

"He's a widower?"

"His wife has left him. There's a daughter, Eve, with her. A younger son, Carleton, is with Mr. Campbell. He has a governess for him."

"Who's the governess?"

"An Englishwoman."

"Who is she? What's her name?"

"Elizabeth Dow."

"All right," Miss Corning said, "get hold of her. Get her on the phone. Dig up some information. I want Endicott Campbell at my suite at the hotel tonight at eight forty-five. Right on the dot, you understand . . . and tell him that I don't like people who are late for appointments. When I say eight forty-five, I mean eight forty-five on the dot.

"Now you get busy on that telephone and I'll put the things I want in these suitcases."

At the end of a full fifteen minutes spent on the telephone Sue knew no more than she had earlier in the day. The foursome at the golf club had been canceled out. Two of the parties to the foursome had joined another pair to make a foursome. They had been advised earlier in the day by Endicott Campbell that he couldn't make it. The other party to the foursome, Harvey Benedict, was an attorney. There was no way that Sue could reach him over the weekend. No residence number was given for him in the telephone book. The phone operator advised her that he had no *listed* residence telephone number.

A telephone call to the Campbell residence brought the information from Elizabeth Dow that the housekeeper had not heard from Endicott Campbell all day; that he was supposed to be home at six thirty; that he had asked to have dinner served promptly at seven o'clock.

When Sue Fisher reported to Miss Corning, the woman sat for nearly thirty seconds motionless in the wheel chair. Her bony face with the high cheekbones, the lantern jaw and the long nose, seemed almost grotesque with the immobility of concentration. Then she said, "Very well. These suitcases are quite heavy for you. Go down and give the man who runs the elevator a couple of dollars to come and take these down to the sidewalk. We'll get a cab there and go to the hotel."

Sue went to the elevator, explained their predicament to the assistant janitor, who promptly came and picked up the suitcases. Then Sue closed up the office and she and Miss Corning went to the elevator and down to the sidewalk. Sue hailed a cab.

"What's your address, my child?" Miss Corning asked.

Sue gave her the address.

"Very well," Miss Corning said to the cab driver, "we'll drive by there first and leave this young woman at her apartment. Then you can take me to the Arthenium Hotel. Now help me fold up this wheel chair."

There was something about the way Miss Corning gave orders

which caused cab drivers instinctively to touch their caps. "Yes, ma'am," he said.

Miss Corning, with deft skill, whipped the wheel chair alongside the open door of the cab. She could, Sue noticed, use her legs enough to be of some assistance as the driver helped her into the cab, but at one period she leaned heavily on Sue's shoulder and it was at that moment Sue got the impression of enormous strength in the long fingers which seemed to dig into her shoulder. Then Miss Corning was in the cab, the wheel chair was being folded and put up in front with the two suitcases. Sue got in the other side of the cab.

"Oh, by the way," Sue said, "I neglected to give you the change from the two hundred dollars. The two suitcases amounted to seventy-six dollars and thirty cents with taxes. And there's the expense money you gave me at the airport."

Sue gave her the receipt, opened her purse to take out the rest of the money.

"Never mind, my child. Forget it," Miss Corning said. "You've had a hard day today. You did nobly and I appreciate it. It's a pleasure to find loyalty in employees. That's a very precious commodity. I don't often find it. You're honest. Did you think I didn't know those first five bills I showed you were hundred-dollar bills? I was testing your honesty. If you'd told me they were tens I'd have fired you on the spot. You are honest; you're loyal; you're a nice girl."

"Why . . . why . . . thank you," Sue said, completely overwhelmed.

"Not at all," Miss Corning said.

"I don't see how you stand it," Sue said. "You must have had a terrific trip flying up from South America and with all the strain of packing and getting away, and the work you've done in the office, and—"

"Bosh!" Miss Corning interrupted curtly. "It was nothing. Don't you worry about me. I stopped over in Miami and had a good hot tub. I'm fresh as a daisy."

"You're sure you don't want me to go to the hotel with you and—"

"What for?" Miss Corning snapped. "I'm perfectly at home there now. I don't like to be babied, young woman. I get along by myself and as you get to know me better you'll find I'm very self-reliant.

"Now, sit back and relax. I want to do some thinking and I don't want to have any chatter. If I want you to say anything I'll ask a question. If I don't ask a question, keep quiet."

"Yes, Miss Corning," Sue said.

They rode in silence until the cab reached Sue's apartment.

"This has been terribly out of your way," Sue said apologetically.

"Not at all. If I'd gone directly to the hotel you wouldn't have taken the cab home. You'd have got out and gone on a bus and been completely exhausted by the time you arrived. As it is now, you can go get into a hot tub and relax. I'm leaving it to you to get in touch with Mr. Campbell and tell him I want to see him at eight forty-five tonight."

"What shall I tell him if he asks about what happened today?"

"Tell him the truth. Never lie to anybody. I don't ask my employees to lie and I don't lie myself. If he asks you questions, answer them."

"But . . . suppose he asks me if you're satisfied? If—"

"Tell him," Miss Corning snapped, "that I said I thought he was a crook. That's what I said and that's what I meant. He's going to have some explaining to do. Good afternoon, Sue."

"Good afternoon, Miss Corning."

Sue got out and stood at the curb, watching the cab drive away with Amelia Corning sitting straight as an arrow in the back seat, her face completely without expression, the dark glasses pointed straight ahead.

Then Sue sighed and took out the latchkey which opened the outer door of the apartment house.

Chapter Two

It was twenty minutes after six when Susan Fisher's phone rang and Endicott Campbell's impatient and irritated voice rasped over the wire.

"What the devil's all this about you calling the golf club and trying to get hold of me, Sue? You know I like to have my weekends undisturbed and I particularly dislike having women telephoning around trying to find out where I am and what I'm doing. Now, what's the trouble?"

Angrily, Susan said, "Well, I like to have a weekend too. I've been working all day and—"

"There is a slight difference in our relative positions," Campbell interrupted, "and," he added pointedly, "in our value to the company. I flatter myself that I am indispensable. You are not. Now start talking."

"In the first place," Sue said, "your son came to the office with a shoe box containing a lot of hundred-dollar bills and said that it was his daddy's treasure, that he and Daddy had traded treasures."

"A what?" Campbell demanded incredulously.

"A shoe box with a lot of hundred-dollar bills in it. It looked pretty well filled."

"You didn't count the money?"

"No."

"You have no idea how much there was in there?"

"There must have been thousands of dollars."

"You mean Carleton had that box?"

"Yes."

"You're crazy!"

"All right," Sue said, "then I'm crazy. But your son had the box and he said it was yours. That's all I know about it."

25

"Where's that box now?"

"I put it in the safe."

"Susan, I can't understand this. I can't . . . Why, I didn't have any treasure . . . I don't know anything about a shoe box filled with hundred-dollar bills. What's the matter? What are you trying to do? My son never gave you any box filled with money. It's impossible! Preposterous!"

"All right. I'm a liar then."

"I wouldn't have put it that bluntly, but you're certainly emotionally disturbed. There's something wrong. You say you put the box with the money in it in the safe?"

"Yes."

"Well, then it'll be there now and we'll try and find out what it's all about. I did let my son play with a box containing a pair of dress shoes. It's preposterous to think there was any money in that box. Now, is that the only reason you had for calling me? This wild tale about my son and a shoe box full of—"

"And Amelia Corning came in on the plane this morning and has been holding me at the office all day, and says that she wants you to call on her promptly at 8:45 and told me to explain that when she said 8:45 she meant—"

"What!" Campbell shouted into the telephone.

"Amelia Corning," Susan said. "She's here."

"She *can't* be here!"

"All right, then I'm lying about that too," she said. "And, if I'm such a little liar I guess there's nothing more I can do, except to say good-by."

She indignantly slammed down the receiver.

She hesitated a moment, then pulled out the telephone directory and looked up the listing of Perry Mason, Attorney at Law.

The directory gave his office address and telephone number with a note in parenthesis, "For night number call Drake Detective Agency."

The number of the Drake Detective Agency was given and Susan dialed the number.

When the switchboard operator at the Drake Detective Agency said, "This is the Drake Detective Agency," Susan was sufficiently nervous to start pouring words into the telephone without giving the operator time to answer.

"I must see Mr. Mason," she said. "I've got to see him tonight at once. This is a very important matter. This is Susan Fisher and I got this number from the telephone directory. It listed it as Mr. Mason's night number and—"

"Just a minute," the operator cut in finally, "and I'll let you talk with Mr. Drake himself. He happens to be here in the office at the moment."

A moment later a man's voice, calm and collected, said, "This is Paul Drake talking. Now, what seems to be the trouble?"

Again Susan Fisher poured words into the line.

Drake started asking questions and almost before she knew it the calm competency of his voice soothed her nerves and she found herself giving a fairly consistent résumé of the events of the day.

"Where are you now?" Drake asked.

She told him.

"All right," Drake said, "I'll try and get in touch with Mr. Mason and call you back. Wait there until you hear from me."

Susan Fisher hung up the telephone, dashed to the bathroom and put fresh powder and rouge on her face, was just touching her mouth with lipstick when the phone rang.

Susan hurried to the phone, picked it up and said, "Yes?" expectantly.

The voice that came over the wire was that of Endicott Campbell.

"Susan," he said, "what the devil! I've been trying to ring you and your line has been busy. I want to get this straight, Susan. *Where* is Miss Corning?"

"At her suite in the Arthenium Hotel."

"That suite was reserved for Monday."

"I know, but it was unoccupied and so she moved in this morning."

"You say she went over company records?"

"She had me up there all day."

"I don't like that."

"I didn't like it either," Sue Fisher said. "She wants to see you at the hotel at exactly eight forty-five."

"Very well," Endicott Campbell said, "and I want to meet you at the office at exactly eight o'clock."

"I don't think I can be there."

"Why not?"

"Because I've been working all day and I'm all in and—and I have an appointment."

"Cancel it."

"I can't be there at eight o'clock."

"Very well," Campbell said. "I will meet you in the lobby of the Arthenium Hotel at eight thirty on the dot. I will give you that much time to break your engagement and straighten out your affairs so that you can cope with the situation in the event of an emergency. If you are not there it will be equivalent to your resignation."

He hung up the phone without saying good-by.

A few moments later the phone rang. It was the soothing, masculine voice again. "Paul Drake talking," the detective said in his calmly matter-of-fact manner. "Mr. Mason and his confidential secretary, Miss Street, are dining at the Candelabra Café. They expect to be finished by eight o'clock. Mr. Mason said that if it is a matter of very great importance he will arrange to see you there at eight."

"But that's right near the Arthenium Hotel!" Susan Fisher exclaimed.

"That's right."

"Oh, I'll be there. I'm so grateful. I . . . Oh, please tell Mr. Mason I can't thank him enough."

Chapter Three

Della Street, looking over the rim of her demitasse cup, said in a low voice, "Unless my judgment of facial expressions is in error, the young woman who just entered the place unescorted and is now standing by the reservations desk is the one who telephoned Paul Drake and is so concerned about the dishonest management of the company where she works."

Mason, who had his back to the entrance, said, "Give me a run-down, Della. While she's waiting, give me the benefit of your feminine appraisal."

"Not bad-looking from a masculine standpoint," Della Street said. "A nice figure, curves in the right places; rather modest, demure—"

"Not from a masculine standpoint," Mason interrupted. "Masculine observations of women are notoriously inaccurate. Let me have it from the feminine viewpoint, Della."

"I don't know how much she makes," Della Street said, "but on a secretarial salary I would say that the clothes she's wearing indicate she's alone in the world. She isn't supporting any mother, father or younger brothers. She knows how to wear her clothes, too. She's neat —what you'd call well-groomed."

"What color hair?"

"Darkish. Not coal black. Sort of a dark chestnut."

"Natural?" Mason asked.

"Heaven knows," Della Street said, "particularly at this distance. You probably couldn't tell anyway."

"Eyes?" Mason asked.

"Rather dark. You can't get the color from here. Either black or dark brown. She's a little lady. She's nervous but making a determined effort to be self-contained. . . . Oh, oh, she's got the headwaiter now. Here she comes."

29

The headwaiter said apologetically, "The young woman says she has an appointment, Mr. Mason."

Mason arose.

Della Street said, "Are you Susan Fisher?" and when the other nodded, extended her hand. "I'm Della Street, Mr. Mason's confidential secretary, and this is Mr. Mason."

"Won't you sit down?" Mason invited.

"I—I'm terribly sorry, Mr. Mason. I shouldn't have disturbed you at dinner but this is a matter of the greatest importance."

"All right," Mason said, "let's hear what it's all about. Would you like a dessert, a liqueur, some coffee? I take it you've dined. . . ."

"Yes. I had a snack—I have to be in the lobby of the Arthenium Hotel in exactly thirty minutes."

"Well, then," Mason said, "perhaps you'd better not waste time with coffee. Just sit down here and tell me everything that happened."

It took Susan Fisher ten full minutes of rapid conversation to describe the events of the day.

When she had finished, Mason's eyes narrowed. He glanced at his wrist watch. "Well," he said, "there isn't time to head things off."

"What do you mean? There's almost twenty minutes. There—"

"No," Mason said, "I meant to get witnesses who can verify the contents of the shoe box."

"You think we should have?"

Mason nodded. "I think you should have had a witness as soon as you discovered what was in the box."

"Why?"

"You don't know how much was in there," Mason said. "Neither does anyone else."

"I know, but the shoe box is intact in the safe."

"Who knows it's intact?"

"Why, I do. I . . ."

Her dismayed voice trailed away into silence.

"Exactly," Mason said. *"You* assume that the box is intact but suppose someone should claim there's two thousand or five thousand dollars missing?"

"Yes," she said. "I see your point."

"Particularly in case that someone should want to discredit you," Mason said.

"And why would anyone want to do that?"

"Because," Mason told her, "apparently you have information about irregularities in the company. Under those circumstances some guilty party might very well try to involve you first."

Mason abruptly signaled the waiter. "I think we'll get over to the Arthenium Hotel as early as possible," Mason told Susan. "Even if Campbell should show up only five minutes early, that would give us an extra five minutes and we may need it."

"Then you'll—you'll represent me?"

Mason nodded. "At least to the extent of looking into it."

She let her fingers close gratefully on his wrist. "Oh, Mr. Mason, I can't tell you what it means to me. I'm beginning to realize . . . Well, this could have quite a blowup and I . . . Gosh, I am in rather a vulnerable position as far as that money is concerned."

"Carleton is too young to have counted it?"

"Heavens, yes."

"How much money would you say was in the box?"

"I don't know. It was a shoe box just crammed full of hundred-dollar bills. That could be quite a large amount, I take it."

Mason nodded. The waiter brought the check. Mason signed it and nodded to Della Street.

"It's only a block," Mason said. "There's no use getting the car out, then trying to find a parking place at the Arthenium. We'll walk."

They left the café and as they walked over to the lobby of the hotel Mason said, "Now, when we walk in, introduce me to Campbell as your lawyer if he's there. If he isn't introduce me to him as soon as he walks in and then let me do the talking."

"He'll resent that," Susan Fisher warned.

"I know he will," Mason said. "But he's going to resent me anyway and I think you need someone to represent you right from the start."

"But after all, Mr. Mason, Miss Corning is the real boss. She's over Mr. Campbell. She's over everyone. She's the one who pays my salary. I thought I should explain that to him and then perhaps we should wait to see if he makes some accusation of—"

"That's not what I'm thinking of at all," Mason said.

"But that's the only reason I wanted you to be there—to tell him that under the law I was not only entitled to do what I did, but obligated to."

Mason said, "I'm thinking of that shoe box full of money."

"Well, it's there in the safe and—"

"And," Mason interrupted, "if Endicott Campbell simply decided to go to the office, open the safe, take out the shoe box full of money and place it where it would never be seen again, you haven't any way on earth of proving that the shoe box was ever there."

"Do you think he'd do that?" she asked.

"I don't know," Mason said, "but when a man has a shoe box full of hundred-dollar bills in his closet I take rather a dim view of his integrity and the Department of Internal Revenue shares my doubts. . . . Well, here we are. Let's go in."

Susan Fisher, speechless with apprehension, walked through the door as Mason held it open for her.

Della Street squeezed Susan's arm with her fingers. "It's all right, Miss Fisher," she said. "Just have confidence in Mr. Mason. He was simply trying to tell you the reason he wanted to conduct the conversation."

"But heavens," Susan Fisher said, "he . . . Of course, Mr. Campbell *wouldn't* do a thing like that, but if he did . . ."

"Exactly," Della Street said. "*If* he did, then what?"

"I don't know," Susan Fisher conceded.

"See him here?" Mason asked, as they looked around the lobby.

She shook her head.

Mason regarded his watch and frowned. "It's a situation where we need every minute we can get. . . . How is he generally on keeping appointments?"

"Quite prompt."

"Well," Mason said, "let's hope he gets here a little early."

Mason glanced at his watch, then began to pace the floor.

"One thing's certain," Susan Fisher said. "He's going to have to be here right on the dot at eight forty-five. That's the time Miss Corning said for him to be here and she explained she didn't want him even as much as a minute late."

They waited until eight thirty-five.

Mason said impatiently, "I want to talk with him before he goes up to see her. I want to see what—"

"Here he comes now," Susan Fisher interrupted, nodding her head toward the entrance to the lobby.

Mason studied the man who came striding toward the elevators: a figure in the late thirties with broad shoulders, a fairly slim waist, a powerful neck, a heavy jaw, thick eyebrows and eyes that seemed strangely intent.

The man came walking toward them and apparently was so pre-occupied that it wasn't until he was within a few feet of Susan Fisher that he noticed her.

"Susan," he said, "what in the world is the meaning of all this? I—"

"I want you to know Mr. Perry Mason, the lawyer," Susan said, "and his secretary, Della Street. Mr. Mason is going to be my lawyer."

If she had pulled out a gun and fired a shot point-blank at Endicott Campbell he couldn't have come to a more abrupt stop or seemed more dismayed.

"An attorney!" he exclaimed.

"Exactly," Mason said, stepping forward and extending his hand. "How are you, Mr. Campbell? I'm representing Susan Fisher."

"But what in the world does *she* need an attorney for?" Endicott Campbell asked.

"That remains to be seen," Mason said. "Did you wish to discuss certain matters with her?"

"I asked her here to discuss certain private business problems and they're problems which affect the company. Some of them are con-fidential. I don't care to have an audience."

Mason, seeing advantage in Campbell's surprise, took the initiative, said, "There was the matter of a shoe box containing some hundred-dollar bills, Mr. Campbell. You seemed to question my client's word about that and that's one of the things I want to have settled."

"That's one of the things *I* want to have settled," Campbell said, turning savagely to face Susan Fisher. "Now then, Susan, what the devil did you mean by trying to hide behind a seven-year-old boy and drag him into your peculations?"

"What in the world are you talking about?" Susan asked.

"You know very well what I mean. This cock-and-bull story you dreamed up about Carleton having a shoe box full of money."

"But he had it."

"Bosh!" Campbell said. "He didn't have any such thing."

"Have you asked him?" Mason inquired.

Campbell whirled to Mason and said, "I don't need to ask him. And as far as I'm concerned *you* have no official status in this party at all."

Mason said, "You have just accused my client of peculations. The accusation was made in the presence of witnesses. Now, just what do you mean by peculations?"

"She knows what I mean," Campbell said, "and I don't think I need to elaborate on it in view of the fact that you quite obviously are simply tagging along here hoping that you can find some grounds for a damage suit. . . . Well, *I'll* tell *you* something, Mr. Perry Mason, you're going to have something a lot more serious to occupy your attention if you're going to represent this young woman."

Campbell turned again to Susan Fisher. "Now then, since you apparently would like to trap me into making accusations I'll simply content myself with asking questions. What about that box of money that you told me about over the telephone?"

"What do you want to know about it?"

"Where did you put it?"

"In the safe."

"And then what did you do with it?"

"Nothing. I left it in the safe."

"Well, it isn't there now," Endicott Campbell said.

"What!" she exclaimed.

"What's more, you know it. . . . All right, I won't make any accusations in view of the fact that you're represented by competent counsel. However, I'll just state this, Susan Fisher, that you told me about having a box of hundred-dollar bills in your possession in the office. Now I'm calling on you to produce that box of hundred-dollar bills."

"I take it," Mason said dryly, "you have already been to the office."

Campbell turned to face him, studied him with hostile eyes and said, "I see no reason to answer that question. On the other hand, I see no reason not to answer the question. I have been to the office. I have opened the safe. I have looked for the box where she said it was and it wasn't there."

"And," Mason said, "what does that prove?"

"It proves she's lying."

"In what way?"

"All right," Campbell said, "I'll put it this way. Let her prove she isn't lying. She didn't have any witnesses as to the amount of money in that box. She didn't even have any witnesses as to the existence of the box."

"And you think she should have?" Mason said.

"It would have been a commendable precaution as far as her veracity is concerned."

"So you went to the office and there wasn't any box in the safe."

"That's right."

"No money, no box?"

"No money, no box."

"And who were *your* witnesses?"

"My witnesses? What do you mean?"

"It would have been a commendable precaution," Mason said.

"Why, you—you—!" Campbell sputtered.

"At some stage of the inquiry," Mason said, "you might be interrogated as to how anyone knows *you* didn't find the box there."

"Well, I didn't, and I think my word is good enough to stand up in any court of law."

"That will depend on several things," Mason said.

"Such as what?" Campbell sneered.

"On the manner in which you're cross-examined," Mason said, "and how you comport yourself on cross-examination. . . . Now, I believe you have an appointment with Amelia Corning?"

"I do."

"And I want to see Amelia Corning," Mason said. He turned to Sue Fisher. "What's her suite, Miss Fisher?"

"The Presidential Suite on the twenty-first floor."

"Then we all may as well go up," Mason said. "I'd like to ask Miss Corning a few questions and I'd also like to make certain that Mr. Campbell doesn't make any insinuations or plant any prejudices in Miss Corning's mind before we have a chance to get a showdown on this."

"You can't come up," Campbell said. "This is a private appointment. This is a matter of business and you have no right to horn in on it."

"And who," Mason asked, "is going to stop me?"

Campbell squared his shoulders, then regarded the rugged features and broad shoulders of the lawyer. "Before you go too far with this thing," he said, "it might interest you to know that I am considered a very good boxer."

"And before *you* go too far with this thing," Mason told him, "it might interest you to know that I'm considered one hell of a good *fighter*."

With that the lawyer turned his back on Campbell and marched toward the elevators.

Della Street took Susan Fisher's arm, followed the lawyer.

Campbell started to follow them, then turned and said, "All right, I'll get the house detective if I have to."

Mason paused for a moment thoughtfully, watching the departing Campbell.

"Will he get the house detective?" Della Street asked.

"I don't know," Mason said, "but first I think he'll go to the room telephones, get Miss Corning and ask her not to see us."

"I'm satisfied she'll see *me*," Susan Fisher said. "She's nice and she likes me. She distrusts him already."

"Well, let's go find out how she feels," Mason suggested.

They entered one of the elevators, went to the twenty-first floor and Susan Fisher led the way down the corridor to the Presidential Suite.

Mason pressed the bell button on the door. They could hear chimes and farther in the interior of the suite they could hear the persistent and intermittent ringing of a telephone bell.

Mason tried the bell buzzer again and knocked at the door. He frowned, said, "She wanted the appointment at eight forty-five, Miss Fisher?"

"That's right, and it was to be on the dot," Susan said.

Mason looked at his watch. "It's twelve minutes to nine now."

"We weren't up here right on the button," Della Street said.

"I have an idea it would be just like her to wait just about thirty seconds, then if Mr. Campbell hadn't shown up to get out of the suite," Susan Fisher said.

"But she has to use a wheel chair?"

"Yes, she can walk a step or two, I think, but she has to hang on to something when she walks. She does nearly everything in the wheel chair."

Mason looked up and down the corridor, was looking toward the elevators when Campbell, accompanied by a quietly dressed, thoughtful-eyed individual, emerged from the elevators and started walking down the corridor.

"This," Mason said, "looks very much like the house detective."

"That isn't the way I thought house detectives looked," Susan Fisher said.

"That," Mason told her smiling, "is the way they all look."

"What way, Mr. Mason?"

"The way people think they *don't* look," Mason said, and stepped forward. "There seems to be no answer in this suite," Mason said to the house detective.

"Should there be?" the man asked.

"We would think so," Mason said.

The man shook his head. "The occupant of this suite checked out a little after five o'clock this afternoon."

"What!" Susan Fisher exclaimed.

"I'm just going to verify the information," the house detective said. "On our books the suite is listed as vacant. The bill was paid in cash and the woman who was in here checked out."

The house detective produced a key from his pocket, said, "I want you folks to notice that I'm not entering a suite that is registered on our books as being occupied. This is a vacant suite. I'm simply going in to look around and inspect the suite to see whether the maids have cleaned up and left soap, towels and clean linen."

The house detective clicked back the lock, swung the door wide, stood aside and bowed to Della Street. "Ladies first," he said.

Della and Susan Fisher entered, followed by Endicott Campbell. Mason and the house detective brought up the rear.

It was a spacious suite, equipped with television, icebox, a little bar with a glassed-in shelf for bottles and glasses, cocktail mixers and a thermidor for ice. There were two bedrooms, two baths, a spacious living room.

The entire suite was not only vacant but in that state of orderly cleanliness which marks vacant hotel rooms.

"That's what I thought," the house detective said.

Campbell was not content with the man's pronouncement. He went prowling around through the bathrooms, looking in odd corners, inspecting the clean towels, even looking on the tile floor of the bathroom.

Suddenly he turned to Susan Fisher and said, "How do we know Miss Corning was here at all?"

Mason caught her eye and warned her to silence. "You might look at the hotel records," he suggested.

"That's exactly what we're going to do," Endicott Campbell said.

"Well, since we're making this a joint investigation," Mason said, "we may as well follow through on it ourselves."

"Now, look here," the house detective interposed, "we don't want to do anything that's going to involve us in any publicity."

"Certainly not," Mason said. "All you want to do is to get the facts so that you *won't* be involved in any publicity."

The house detective narrowed his eyes. "How do you know the facts won't involve us in any publicity?"

"I don't," Mason said cheerfully. "However, I'm assuming that *you* haven't anything to conceal and I know *we* haven't anything to conceal. I'm sure Endicott Campbell hasn't anything to conceal."

"I don't like that. I object to the insinuation," Campbell said.

"What insinuation?" Mason said.

"That I have anything to conceal."

"I specifically said you didn't have."

"Well, I'm not going to argue with you. Come on, let's go down to the desk and see what the records show."

They left the suite, went down to the registration desk, and the house detective explained the situation to the registration clerk.

The man at the desk spoke guardedly. "I wasn't on duty this morning. I understand that when this party came in she was in a wheel chair and was accompanied by a young woman who signed the register at the request of Miss Corning. The suite had been re-served for her, although it was reserved for Monday morning instead of this morning. I have talked with the clerk who was on duty this morning. I understand he asked her how long she was going to be here and she said probably two or three weeks. The young woman who was with her was the one who signed the register."

"That was I," Susan Fisher said. "She asked me to sign for her because she was in her wheel chair."

"Wasn't that highly irregular?" Campbell asked the clerk.

"It was unusual," the clerk conceded. "It wasn't irregular in view of Miss Corning's prominence and the fact that she intended to be here for a while. . . . Of course, as I say, I wasn't on duty at the time. I understand quite a few people were checking in, baggage was piled up in the lobby and a woman in a wheel chair is certainly entitled to some consideration."

"She seems to have received plenty," Campbell said dryly.

"What we're interested in," Mason said, "is what happened afterward. Do you know about that?"

"I'll have to refer you to the cashier. I was on duty when she checked out. I saw her going out and I wondered if she might be checking out but then dismissed it because our reservation list showed she was going to be here some little time."

"She did have suitcases with her?" Mason asked.

"She had baggage with her, yes."

The clerk called the assistant manager who in turn got in touch with the cashier. It appeared that Miss Corning had checked out shortly after five o'clock that afternoon.

Mason led the way from the cashier's desk to the doorman, who regarded the folded bill which Mason pressed into his hand with respectful attention.

"A woman with dark glasses, in a wheel chair," Mason said, "checked out somewhere around five o'clock and . . ."

"Oh, yes, yes, I remember her. I remember her very well."

"Did she leave in a private car, or in a taxicab?"

"A taxicab."

"Do you know which one?"

"No, I don't. I don't remember the man. . . . Now, wait a minute, I do, too. I remember his face. I don't remember the cab but I remember the driver. He's here quite frequently and . . . Now, wait a minute. I saw him back here in line a little while ago. He's . . . Let's take a look down the line here. I think he's the fourth or fifth cab in line."

They walked rapidly down the sidewalk in a compact group. The doorman stopped in front of a cab, said, "Yes, this is the one."

The cab driver seemed somewhat apprehensive. "What is it?" he asked, lowering the window of the cab.

Mason said, "We're trying to locate a woman who left here in a wheel chair about five o'clock. She went in your cab and . . ."

"Oh, yes," the driver said. "I took her down to the Union Station."

"And then what?"

"I don't know. She paid me off and got a redcap."

"She was taking a train somewhere?"

"I think so, yes."

"Well," Mason said, "that seems to be all we can do at this end." He thanked the cab driver, turned back toward the entrance to the hotel.

Endicott Campbell waited a second or so, then forged rapidly ahead to come abreast of the attorney. "Look here, Mason," he said. "Has it ever occurred to you that this woman was carrying away with her records of the corporation; records which are confidential and which are exceedingly important; records which the corporation must have; records which should *never* have been taken from the office of the corporation?"

"How much of the corporation's stock does Miss Corning own?" Mason asked.

"About ninety per cent," Campbell said.

Mason smiled at him, *"That's* your answer."

"Now, wait a minute," Campbell told him belligerently. *"That's* not the answer. You can't dismiss something like that with a wisecrack."

"Why not?"

"Because I'm responsible for the records."

"Then I'll put it another way," Mason said. "To whom are you responsible?"

"The stockholders."

"Now then," Mason said, "I'll ask you again. How much stock does Amelia Corning own?"

"Oh, the devil!" Campbell said, and turning on his heel walked quickly away.

Mason grinned at the house detective, shook hands, said, "I think we can handle this thing all right so there'll be no publicity."

"You do the best you can," the house detective said. "You know things of that sort don't look good in the papers. We're running a very conservative hotel here and—"

"I understand," Mason said. "We'll do all we can to co-operate with you and—"

Mason let his voice cease abruptly.

The house detective grinned, "Sure, sure. *We'll* co-operate with *you,* too, Mr. Mason. Anything you want, you just call on me. The name's Bailey. Colton, C-o-l-t-o-n C. Bailey. You just ask for me and I'll do anything I can."

"Thanks a lot," Mason told him, and turned to the two young women. "Let's go finish our dinner," he said, and led the way back toward the Candelabra Café.

"Oh, I beg a thousand pardons," Susan Fisher said. "I thought you had finished your dinner."

"We had," Mason said, "but I didn't want the house detective to know just where we were going."

"Where *are* you going?"

"To my office," Mason said. "We're going to get Paul Drake on the trail of Amelia Corning and we're going to try to reach her before Endicott Campbell does. When Endicott Campbell left I feel certain he was planning to do a little amateur detective work of his own. Unless I miss my guess he's on his way to the Union Depot right now and when he gets there he'll start checking with the various redcaps, trying to find out just what happened."

"Then aren't you afraid he's beating you to the punch?" Susan Fisher asked.

"Not necessarily," Mason told her. "There are ways of going about these things. Up in the office we have a timetable. We'll check what trains were pulling out at about that time. We'll get Paul Drake to put some professionals on the job and we'll find out what tickets were sold. Campbell may find out where she went after she got to the Union Depot before we do, but I'll bet we find out where she is now before Endicott Campbell does. That is, unless he's shrewd enough to hire professional detectives."

"And then what?"

"Then," Mason said, "we'll wait in my office until we get some definite word. A woman who is nearly blind and confined to a wheel chair can't simply vanish into thin air."

The lawyer retrieved his car from the restaurant parking attendant. They drove to Mason's office. Della Street rang Paul Drake and asked him to come to the office.

A few moments later Paul Drake's peculiarly spaced knock sounded on the door of Mason's private office and Della Street let the detective in.

Mason said, "Paul, this is Susan Fisher. She's an employee of the

Corning Mining, Smelting and Investment Company. The company is pretty much a one-man outfit that's owned by Amelia Corning, a wealthy woman who's been living in South America.

"Miss Corning is about fifty-five years old, nearly blind, wears very large-lensed dark blue glasses, and apparently because of arthritis has to spend most of her time in a wheel chair. She was at the Arthenium Hotel. She checked out shortly after five o'clock, and took a cab to the Union Depot."

Drake, his manner indolent to the point of suggesting chronic laziness, listened with a bland expression which masked the professional competence with which he was sizing up Susan Fisher.

"What do you want done?" he asked Mason.

"Find her," Mason said.

Drake walked quietly toward the outer office. "I'll use the phone in your reception room, if you don't mind. It won't disturb you so much."

Drake gave Susan Fisher a vaguely reassuring smile, vanished into the outer office.

"He's good?" Sue Fisher asked.

"The best," Mason said.

Drake returned to the private office after some ten minutes, said, "I've been playing tunes on your telephone, Perry. I've got men on the job. I've got men covering the taxi companies and broadcasting inquiries over their communications system asking for information. I'll have three men at the depot within ten minutes, probably less. They'll be interrogating the cab starter, the redcaps; inquiring at the ticket windows."

"Good work, Paul," Mason said.

Della Street handed a neatly typewritten piece of paper to Paul Drake. "These are the scheduled trains on both Southern Pacific and Santa Fe leaving after four P.M. tonight."

Paul Drake folded the paper, slipped it in his pocket, said, "Thanks, Della." And then added, after a moment, "Great minds run in the same channel."

"Meaning you've already checked on the timetables?" Mason asked.

"Meaning the first thing my men will do when they reach the depot after giving it a quick once-over to see if she's still there in the waiting room will be to find the outgoing trains. If she's on a train, Perry, I take it you'd like to know where she is before the train reaches its destination."

"That's right," Mason said.

"Any ideas?" Drake asked.

Mason said, "There's a train that goes up to Sacramento. It goes through Mojave. I wouldn't be at all surprised if the person we want was a passenger to Mojave."

"Good heavens!" Sue Fisher exclaimed. "I'll bet that's *exactly* what she did."

"If she waited for that train," Della Street said, "she would have been in the waiting room for some little time."

Mason nodded.

"Any ideas why she would have checked out of the hotel and gone to the depot in order to put in the time waiting in a public waiting room when she could have put in the time just as well in a luxurious suite of the Arthenium?"

"Now, wait a minute," Drake said, "you're going at this thing all backwards. You're starting out with a surmise and then trying to fit facts to it. Now, let's first find out the facts, and *then* we'll make our surmises afterwards—okay?"

"Okay," Mason said, grinning.

"All right," Drake assured them, "I'm going down to my office and start handling calls from there."

He left the office and Sue Fisher turned uneasily to Mason. "You haven't asked me for money yet."

"That's right, I haven't," Mason told her, smiling.

"I'm a working girl on a salary, Mr. Mason, and—Well, I didn't want to say anything in front of Mr. Drake, but I simply can't afford all these detectives and all of this high-priced action."

"That's all right," Mason told her. "Right at the present time this is my party."

"But even so, Mr. Mason, I just haven't got enough—"

"Miss Corning has money," Mason interposed.

She raised puzzled eyebrows.

Mason merely smiled.

After a few moments, Sue Fisher said, "But, Mr. Mason, Miss Corning isn't going to pay for my legal expenses."

"Certainly not," Mason told her. "But I think we may be helping Miss Corning do something that she wants to do very much indeed. This makes for a very interesting situation."

Della Street smiled at Susan Fisher and said, "Just get a magazine from the outer office and make yourself comfortable. We have work to do and we're going to have to utilize every minute."

Della Street went to her office and presently the keyboard of her typewriter exploded into noise. Mason picked up a copy of the "Advance Decisions," said to Sue Fisher, "I'm so busy that it's awfully hard to keep up on these new decisions. If it weren't for moments like these I wouldn't ever be able to catch up."

Sue nodded, went to the waiting room, then tiptoed back with several magazines. She tried to read for a while, then, finding herself too excited to get lost in the printed page, left the magazines on her lap and sat quietly watching Mason's face, noticing that his concentration was so great that he seemed to have completely dismissed her from his mind.

The phone shattered the silence within thirty minutes after Paul Drake had left the room. Della Street, hurrying to the telephone, said, "Hello," then said, "Yes, what is it, Paul?"

She listened with a frown, then said, "I think you'd better come down. . . . Yes, she's still here."

Della Street hung up the telephone and said, "Paul's coming down. They've uncovered a peculiar situation."

"I thought perhaps they would," Mason said, putting down the paper-backed "Advance Decisions."

Della Street moved over to stand by the door.

"He has his offices on this floor?" Susan Fisher asked.

Mason nodded.

Drake's knock sounded on the door and Della Street had the door open with the first touch of the detective's knuckles.

"Well?" Mason asked, as Drake entered the room.

Drake shook his head. "Something goofy, Perry."

"What?"

"All right," Drake said, "here's what happened. She made no attempt to cover up on her arrival at the depot. She attracted a *lot* of attention. She had four suitcases. Two of them were very heavy, as though they contained books of some sort."

"Or bottles," Mason said, grinning.

"Or bottles," Drake admitted. "Somehow the redcap thought they were books.

"She wanted the suitcases put in some of the key lockers, where you drop a quarter, put in the suitcase, close the door, turn the key and walk away."

Mason nodded.

"She got rid of all the suitcases, gave the porter a good tip and then went whizzing along on her wheel chair toward the ladies' room —and completely disappeared."

"Didn't enter the ladies' room?" Mason asked.

"No one knows. From that point she just vanished into thin air."

"You covered the trains?"

"Train dispatchers, redcap porters, ticket sellers, everybody. We got the redcap porter who had put the suitcases in the lockers for her to point out the lockers. We got one of the locker superintendents with a passkey to open them."

"Empty?" Mason asked.

"Empty," Drake said.

"That," Mason said, "is what I was afraid of."

"What?" Susan Fisher asked.

Mason's face hardened. "I told you," he said, "that a woman of fifty-five, with dark blue glasses, a woman who is almost blind and confined to a wheel chair couldn't go to a public place like the Union Depot and simply disappear into thin air."

"I know you did," Sue Fisher said, "but—"

Mason smiled as she broke off.

Sue Fisher went on, "But she seems to have done it?"

Mason turned to Paul Drake. "Paul," he said, "I want you to close up every possible avenue out of that Union Depot. I want your men to get to work and cover everything. *Everything,* you understand? I want to know every way by which a person could leave that depot, and I want every one of those ways checked. I don't care if they have to stay on the job all night."

"Will do," Drake promised, and left the office.

Sue Fisher said, "Can you tell me what you're afraid of, Mr. Mason?"

Mason said, "A woman of that sort couldn't vanish into thin air. Therefore, if she *did* vanish into thin air, we have to start out with the idea that our premise is wrong."

"You mean that she couldn't do what she actually did?"

"No," Mason said, "I mean that she wasn't a woman of that description."

"You mean . . . ? Are you trying to tell me that . . . ?"

"Suppose," Mason suggested, "this woman was an impostor? You don't *know* Amelia Corning. *You're* the only one who saw her. She called you and said she was Amelia Corning. She looked like the Amelia Corning you've had described to you. You went down to the airport. She was sitting there surrounded with luggage with South American labels—that alone may be a significant fact."

"What do you mean?"

Mason said, "Under ordinary circumstances, the baggage would have been held in the checkroom of the airport. This woman was sitting in the lobby in a wheel chair. She had the baggage around her. Now, how did she get it there? Obviously she didn't go and pick up the baggage and carry it in a wheel chair. Therefore, she must have had a porter bring it to her.

"Now, why would she have done that? It would have been far more logical for her to have left the baggage stored in the baggage room until she had her transportation ready and then she'd let the porter take it out to the place where her transportation was waiting.

"The idea of a woman sitting right in the middle of the lobby in a wheel chair with baggage piled around her and that baggage ostentatiously plastered with labels of South American hotels indicates that she was very, very anxious to have you identify her the moment you walked in and to take her for granted.

"That thing bothered me," Mason said, "when you told me about it. But afterward, after you described her character, I came to the conclusion she might be just the sort of person who would insist on keeping her baggage under her eye, so I tried to dismiss the thought from my mind. However, that's one of the reasons I've been worried about this case."

"Then you yourself feel the woman was an impostor?"

"I don't know," Mason said. "I do know that from the minute you told me about her sitting there in the airport with the luggage around her I began to consider that as a possibility.

"Now, if she's an impostor, you must admit she made a pretty good haul. She got away with a lot of incriminating evidence against Endicott Campbell, which would give her good grounds for blackmail, and she probably got away with a shoe box containing heaven knows how many thousands of dollars and—"

Mason was interrupted by a half-scream of apprehension. Susan Fisher, her face white, her eyes wide, pressed knuckles to her mouth. There was no mistaking the expression of utter dismay on her face.

"So you see," Mason said, "I didn't want to talk fees for a while. I wanted to find out what this was all about. And I don't want you to get trapped so there isn't any avenue of escape."

Sue Fisher managed to blurt out, "What do you mean about your premise being wrong?"

Mason said, "Let's assume that this woman who had been posing as Amelia Corning was an impostor. Let's assume she went to the ladies' room, stepped out of the wheel chair, took off the dark glasses, then walked back out to the entrance not as a helpless cripple, but as a vigorous woman."

"And someone met her?" Sue Fisher asked.

"Someone must have met her," Mason said. "Someone who opened the lockers, took out the suitcases, put them in a car, folded the wheel chair, put it in the trunk of the car, then drove the woman who had been posing as Miss Corning out into the city where there is nothing to distinguish one middle-aged woman from a million others."

"She *must* have taken that box," Sue Fisher said in a dismayed whisper.

"She certainly *could* have," Mason said. "Now then, Miss Fisher, I want you to go home. I want you to *try* not to worry. In the event there are any developments of any nature that have any bearing on the case, I want you to call the Drake Detective Agency and leave a message."

Mason arose, put his hand on her arm, led her gently to the door. "You can get home all right?"

She said, "Of course. All I do is get on a bus, then walk three blocks and I'm home."

"Three blocks?" Mason asked.

She nodded.

"How much money do you have?"

"Oh, I have some money left over from what Miss Corning gave me. Did you want a retainer?"

"No," Mason said. "I want you to treat yourself to a taxicab.

Have it deposit you right at the door of your apartment. *Don't* leave your apartment at night under any circumstances until after you have called Paul Drake and cleared with him."

The lawyer walked down the corridor with her to the elevators. After she had taken the elevator, he turned back to Paul Drake's office. There was no longer any reassuring smile on his face as he faced the detective.

"Okay, Paul," he said, "keep your men on at the depot, but get some additional men down at the airport. Keep them there."

Drake frowned. "You mean you expect Miss Corning to show up down there?"

Mason nodded.

"You think she took a cab to the depot, then detoured back to the airport and is leaving . . . ?"

"Hell, no," Mason said. "I think she's *coming.*"

It took a moment for the significance of what Mason said to dawn on the detective. Then he said, "Oh-oh! What a mess *this* is going to be!"

Mason said, "Apparently the route she'll use is to fly to Miami, then take a plane from Miami here. That's the route this other woman *claimed* she took, so that's probably the route Miss Corning is going to take. She'll clear with Immigration and Customs at Miami, then come on through here.

"You get men to cover the airport and let me know the minute she arrives—and I mean the *minute* she arrives here—no matter what hour of the day or night. I don't want her to have an opportunity to get near a telephone or do anything before I see her. Have one of your men approach her, tell her that he's been assigned to meet her. He doesn't need to say whether it's the company that has given him the instructions. He can just make the general statement that he's been assigned to meet her. He can say he'll escort her to the hotel. Then have him get me on the phone right away."

"You'll go to the airport?" Drake asked.

"There won't be time," Mason said, "I'll be waiting at the Arthenium Hotel when she arrives."

"And what about Endicott Campbell?"

"Endicott Campbell is making this a battle of wits," Mason said. "If he can anticipate what's going to happen he can meet us on an equal footing. Otherwise, I'm going to talk with her first."

"And Susan Fisher?" Drake asked.

"Within two hours after Miss Corning shows up," Mason said, "Sue Fisher will be arrested for embezzlement of probably as much as a hundred and fifty thousand dollars. She'll be charged with having spirited away the books and vouchers of the corporation so that there can't be any actual audit, and be in trouble up to her neck."

Drake thought that over for a minute, then lugubriously shook his head. "And even you can't think up any defense that'll get her out of that trap," he said.

"Don't be too sure, Paul," Mason told him. "*You* start running interference and *I'll* carry the ball. But I want some damn *good* interference. Now get started."

Chapter Four

Sunday morning at eleven thirty Mason's unlisted phone rang and Paul Drake's voice came over the wire.

"Okay, Perry, you win."

"She's here?"

"At the airport. My man's getting things all lined up for her and he's going to take her to the Arthenium in an agency car."

"Okay, Paul, thanks," Mason said. "I'm on my way."

"You want me there?"

"No. Ring up Della's apartment, ask her to get there as fast as she can. Tell her to bring a notebook and her feminine charm. Something seems to tell me this woman may be a little suspicious of men, but Della should be able to win her over. At least she can try."

"Okay," Drake said. "I'll wish you luck, Perry."

"I'll need it," the lawyer said.

Mason called Susan Fisher's apartment. "I'm just alerting you," he said.

"For what?"

"To be ready for action."

"What sort of action?"

"I may want you to go someplace."

"All right," she told him, "I'll be ready. Anything you say, Mr. Mason."

"Keep near the telephone and be dressed to go out," Mason said, and hung up. He got his car from the garage, drove to the Arthenium Hotel and waited for fifteen minutes before Drake's detective showed up solicitously squiring an angular woman in a wheel chair, a woman who wore glasses with large blue lenses, who had high cheekbones, a prominent jaw and a firm mouth.

Mason approached the woman. "Miss Corning?" he asked.

She raised her head and moved it from side to side, peering from behind the heavy blue glasses, trying to get some picture of the man whose voice she had heard.

Then, after a moment, she answered shortly, "I'm Miss Corning. What is it you want?"

"I'm Perry Mason," the lawyer said. "I'm an attorney and I want to talk with you on a matter of the greatest importance, a matter concerning your holdings here. I think it's quite important that you hear what I have to say before you get in touch with anyone."

She hesitated a moment, then said, "Very well, I'll be glad to hear what you have to say, Mr. Mason. I believe a suite has been arranged for me here. At least that's the information I've been given by wire."

"I understand your company is expecting you," Mason said.

"Well, they did a better job of it than I thought they could. But I still don't know how they found out when I was coming. I am not scheduled to appear officially until tomorrow. However, the trip up is a long, hard one and I decided I'd get here a day early, just stretch my weary bones out and rest."

Drake's operative, who had approached the desk, came over to the wheel chair with a registration card and the desk clerk.

The operative glanced significantly at Mason and said, "The hotel wants Miss Corning's *personal* signature on the registration card."

"Certainly," Mason said.

Miss Corning stretched out a bony hand, reached for the card which the clerk was handing her, but her fingers were some six or eight inches over the card.

The clerk tactfully withdrew the card, then pushed it right into her fingers.

"Just sign here," the clerk said.

"Where?" Miss Corning asked, holding the pen.

"Right here." The clerk put his hand over hers, touched the pen to the paper and the woman immediately wrote "Amelia Corning" in an angular, cramped but legible handwriting.

A bellboy said, "Right this way, Miss Corning."

"You only have the two suitcases and a handbag?" Mason asked.

"Good heavens, how much did you expect? Do you know what excess baggage costs on those planes coming up from South America? It's highway robbery . . . I wish now I'd only brought the one bag

. . . of course, comfort is something, but, after all, a dollar's a dollar. Now, let's go up and find out what it is you want, Mr. . . . er . . ."

"Mason," the lawyer prompted.

"Oh, yes, Mason. All right, I'm not much good at names but I'll try and remember. You have a nice voice. I think I'm going to like you."

The lawyer walked beside the wheel chair as they approached the elevators.

Colton C. Bailey, the house detective, who had evidently been alerted by the clerk, appeared on the screen, shook hands with Mason, said quietly, "Introduce me."

Mason said, "Miss Corning, may I present Mr. Colton Bailey. He's connected here with the hotel in an executive capacity and if there's anything you want he'll be only too glad to try and see that you are accommodated."

"That's very nice," Miss Corning said. "I'll go up and take a look around at that Presidential Suite. The probabilities are I'll want to be moved into something more modest. There's no need for me to be rattling around in a lot of room I don't need, and those suites cost money."

"We'll go up right now and take a look, Miss Corning," Bailey said. "We want to be certain you're satisfied."

The little entourage went up to the Presidential Suite. The bellboy opened the door and Bailey, Mason and Drake's operative wheeled Miss Corning into the main room.

She looked around and sniffed. "I'll bet this costs a hundred dollars a day," she said.

"A hundred and thirty-five," Bailey said apologetically.

"All right, I want to move out and get into something smaller."

"The rental has been arranged, I believe," Bailey said.

She sniffed. "That's Endicott Campbell for you. Spending company funds on a luxury that I don't need, trying to impress me. By the way, where *is* he?"

Bailey looked at Mason inquiringly.

Mason glanced at his watch and said, "Apparently he hasn't arrived yet, Miss Corning, but you can probably expect him."

Bailey said, "Now, Miss Corning, there's a certain formality that we have to go through on account of security reasons. You'll probably be wanting to cash checks here at the hotel and we'd like to establish a line of credit. Of course, the financial end of it is all taken care of; all we need is a complete check on identity. I'm wondering if you'd mind letting me see your passport."

"Humph!" she said. "I haven't asked you for anything yet except smaller quarters."

"But," he said, "if it's all the same to you, we'd like to see your passport, Miss Corning."

"Well, of all things!" she said. "I've been showing that damn passport . . . I was hoping that when I got to my own country I wouldn't need to wear it on my sleeve and keep showing it to every Tom, Dick and Harry that would ask for it."

Suddenly she realized how her remark sounded and gave a frosty smile. "Not that you're Tom or Dick or Harry . . . or are you?"

"No, Miss Corning," Bailey said. "I'm Colton. Colton Bailey."

"Oh, all right," she said. "I'm glad you took it in good part. I guess my nerves are a little frayed."

She opened her purse and took out a passport.

Bailey carefully inspected the passport, then nodded to Mason as he returned the passport to Miss Corning.

"Well," he said, with a voice that plainly showed his relief, "there's nothing more I can do here, Miss Corning; at least at the moment. I'll withdraw and leave you and Mr. Mason to talk things over."

Drake's operative said, "And I have discharged my duties, Miss Corning. I guess there is nothing else you need of me."

As they opened the door, Della Street, neatly tailored, calmly efficient, came walking into the room.

She sized up the situation, moved over to the chair and said, "How do you do, Miss Corning? I'm Della Street. I'm Mr. Mason's executive secretary and Mr. Mason asked me to come here so that I could be of any assistance possible. In case there's anything that's in the feminine department I want to do all I can to make you comfortable."

Miss Corning twisted her head with a distinctive, birdlike gesture, tilting it from one side to the other as though hoping to get a better view through the heavy lenses.

"Well, my dear," she said, "I can't see you very clearly, but I can see you have a very trim figure and your voice is wonderful. As my eyes get worse, I depend more on my ears. I rely a *great* deal on voices. I certainly like yours."

"Thank you. Thank you very much indeed," Della Street said.

"Not at all. Now, Mr. Mason, you're a lawyer. If your time isn't valuable you aren't a very good lawyer. If you're a very good lawyer your time is worth a lot of money. Neither of us wants to waste it. So let's get to the point."

"Wouldn't you like to freshen up first?" Mason asked.

"You go right ahead, young man," she snapped. "You'll find I'm fresh enough. Now, just what is it you want?"

"It's not what I want," Mason said. "It's something one of my clients wants."

"Well, it's the same thing," she told him. "Now, go on. Start talking. Sit down, make yourself comfortable and have that delightful young secretary of yours make herself comfortable."

"You're all right in the wheel chair?" Della Street asked. "You don't want to move into a more comfortable chair?"

"I'm all right, right here," Miss Corning said.

Mason said, "I'm not going to take the time to try to be diplomatic, Miss Corning. In a matter of this sort, I have only one approach and that is to put the cards right on the table."

"Face up," Miss Corning said.

"Face up," Mason said, smiling. "Now, the first thing that I have to tell you, and which may come as something of a shock to you, is that yesterday a woman who claimed to be you appeared at the airport and telephoned the offices of the Corning Mining, Smelting and Investment Company."

"What!" she exclaimed.

Mason nodded.

"Well, go on," Miss Corning said. "What happened?"

"There," Mason said, "we get into the realm of speculation. I can't tell you exactly what happened. However, I can tell you this much. This woman telephoned the company offices. A young woman by the name of Susan Fisher, who acts as confidential secretary to Endicott Campbell, the manager, and who was called up by Mr. Campbell to get certain things in readiness for your arrival, was working overtime there and answered the telephone.

"Upon being advised that Miss Corning was at the airport, that a telegram had been sent announcing an earlier date of arrival and upon being unable to get in touch with Mr. Campbell, she dashed out to the airport.

"There she found a woman who apparently had a very striking physical resemblance to you seated in a wheel chair, surrounded by baggage bearing the labels of South American hotels and South American airlines. She escorted this woman to this suite of rooms and the woman insisted on going almost immediately to the office in order to check into certain things."

"What happened?" Miss Corning asked.

"This woman showed a surprising familiarity with the business. She inquired about various details, then she sent Susan Fisher down to buy some suitcases and put certain vouchers and books of account in those suitcases and then vanished. There *is* a possibility that she took with her a fairly large sum of money from the safe. We can't be certain about that."

"Why can't you be certain about it?"

"Because the origin of that money is shrouded in a certain amount of mystery."

"All right," Miss Corning said, "where do *you* come in?"

"I'm representing Susan Fisher."

"Does she need an attorney?"

"She may need an attorney."

"Why?"

"Because," Mason said, "she may have let an impostor into the office; she may have been the victim of an impersonation and turned over certain vouchers and books of account and permitted them to leave the office."

"Why all that hurried activity on a Staurday?" Miss Corning asked.

"Frankly," Mason said, "because there is some reason to believe that there may have been irregularities in the operation of the company. Take, for instance, the mine in the Mojave Desert known as the Mojave Monarch. That mine—"

"That mine," Miss Corning interrupted firmly, "needs looking into. You don't need to go on to tell me any more about that, Mr. Mason. That's one of the reasons I'm here. Now then, where's Endicott Campbell?"

"I don't know," Mason said. "Frankly, I was somewhat anticipating your arrival at the airport and the man who met you was one who is in my employ rather than in the employ of the company."

"And you think somebody is going to make trouble for this young woman client of yours?"

"Mr. Campbell has indicated as much."

"All right," Miss Corning said, "let's get hold of Mr. Campbell and let's get hold of this young woman. Where's this very efficient secretary of yours? Is she here?"

"Right here," Della Street said.

"All right," Miss Corning said. "I presume you know the number of your client's telephone. Here are some numbers that Mr. Campbell gave me where *he* can be reached in case he's not at home. However, this is his home number and you can try that first. Now, let's get both of them up here."

Della Street started putting through the telephone calls.

Mason said, "Of course, Miss Corning, in view of your large holdings in the company, regardless of what Mr. Campbell may feel should be done, the ultimate fate of Susan Fisher rests very largely in your hands."

"That's right," Miss Corning said. "You don't need to waste time pointing out the obvious to me, Mr. Mason. That's why I want to get her up here. My eyes aren't too good, but I'm a pretty good judge of voices. Now that I can't see so well, I have to make up for it by listening. After I hear a person talk I can tell whether I want to trust that person or not. My judgment isn't infallible but it suits me all right.

"And I'll tell you something else. The reason I'm here is that I called up Endicott Campbell on international long-distance telephone and I didn't like the sound of *his* voice. There was a certain equivocation in his voice that I didn't like. I don't know what's happening. I don't know whether he's trying to protect himself or someone else, but . . . well, I'm here to find out."

Della Street reported, "Endicott Campbell isn't at home. The housekeeper who is there doesn't know where he is. She's there alone. Elizabeth Dow, the governess, Carleton Campbell, the young son, and Endicott Campbell, are all out somewhere."

"Together?" Mason asked.

"She doesn't know," Della Street said.

"What about Susan Fisher, Della?"

"I got Miss Fisher on the line and told her to get up here right away. She's coming up immediately."

"All right," Miss Corning said. "Now, I'm going to do this freshening up you were talking about. If this secretary of yours, Mr. Mason, wouldn't mind assisting a somewhat helpless old woman, we'll retire to one of the bedrooms. You can sit here in the room which I believe is still known as a parlor in hotel lingo. I don't want to have anyone else around. Just sit here and wait, Mr. Mason, and I'll be out shortly. In the meantime, if that young woman client of yours comes in, just tell her to sit down and be comfortable, and that we'll be out before too very long.

"Now then," she said, turning to Della, "*your* name is Della Street?"

"That's right," Della said.

"Would you mind coming in the bedroom with me and helping me unpack? My eyes are just no good at all and it's difficult to unpack by feeling. . . . Oh, I can see outlines and get a vague impression of faces, but bright light bothers me and I can't see anything in a half-light. I'm getting worse all the time. I have to rely more and more on a sense of touch."

"I'll be glad to do anything I can to help," Della Street said.

"You have loyalty and efficiency," Miss Corning announced, "and unless I'm very much mistaken, you have a great deal of ability. Come along now."

The women retired to the bedroom. Mason settled back in one of the comfortable chairs, tried to relax but couldn't, then got up and started thoughtfully pacing the floor.

The lawyer was still pacing when knuckles tapped gently on the outer door. Mason opened it and a frightened Susan Fisher stood in the hallway.

"Come in," Mason said.

She entered the room, looking around apprehensively.

"They're in the bedroom unpacking and Miss Corning is freshening up," Mason said.

"How bad is it?" Sue Fisher asked.

"Not bad at all—at least not so far. Miss Corning is a very well-balanced, unemotional woman who gives the impression of being most considerate."

"Has Mr. Campbell got hold of her yet?"

"No," Mason said. "As far as I know, Campbell has no idea that she is in the city. He's expecting her tomorrow."

"How did *you* know she was here?"

Mason grinned and said, "I anticipated it."

"What do you mean?"

"Well," Mason said, "I knew she was due to arrive tomorrow and I thought she *might* arrive a day ahead of time. So Paul Drake had men at the airport waiting for her to arrive. When she showed up, Drake's man stepped forward and met her and told her he'd take charge of her baggage and promptly proceeded to notify Paul Drake, who, in turn, notified me. And here we are."

"You mean you thought all that out in advance?"

"There wasn't anything much to think out in advance," Mason said. "We knew that Miss Corning was going to show up at the airport and I wanted to have an opportunity to tell her your side of the story before Endicott Campbell told her his side of the story. That's all there was to it."

Susan Fisher impulsively took Mason's hand in both of hers. "I think you're absolutely wonderful," she said. "Why didn't you tell me what you were doing?"

"I was afraid you might worry," Mason said. "I wanted you to get a good night's sleep. Did you?"

"I slept off and on," she said, "but it wasn't what you'd call a good night's sleep. Do I look a wreck?"

"You look wonderful," Mason told her. "But Miss Corning doesn't depend too much on her eyes. She depends a great deal on her ears. She likes to listen to persons' voices when they talk and makes an appraisal of character from those voices. She—"

The bedroom door opened and Della Street pushed Miss Corning's wheel chair out into the room.

"Hello, Susan," Della Street said. "This is Miss Corning. Miss Corning, Susan Fisher is here."

"Where are you, child?" Miss Corning asked.

"Right here," Sue said, coming forward to the chair. "Oh, Miss Corning, I feel so terrible about what happened yesterday. Mr. Mason says he's told you the facts."

"Sit down here close to me," Miss Corning said, "and tell me what happened."

Della Street said. "I'll wheel Miss Corning over here by this chair, Susan, then you can talk with her on one side and Mr. Mason will be on the other."

Miss Corning said, "I suppose this isn't very ethical, Mr. Mason, but I would like to steal your secretary. I don't know what Mr. Mason is paying you, Miss Street, but I'll double it."

"Now just a minute," Mason interposed. "This is criminal conspiracy, grand larceny and treason."

"No such thing," Miss Corning said. "It's a business proposition and there's no treason involved because I don't owe you any loyalty. Miss Street is the only one who owes you any loyalty and she wouldn't even consider such a proposition. Would you, Della?"

"I'm afraid not," Della Street said, laughing.

"Well, let's get down to business. Now then, young lady . . . what's your name—Fisher?"

"That's right, Susan Fisher."

"How old are you, Susan?"

"Twenty-four."

"Good figure?"

Susan laughed in an embarrassed manner and Della Street said, "Very good, Miss Corning."

"In love?" Miss Corning asked.

"Not at the moment."

"How long have you been working in the office there?"

"More than a year."

"Did you start in as Mr. Campbell's secretary?"

"No. I started in as a stenographer."

"He picked you out to become his secretary?"

"Yes."

"How good are you at typing?"

"I'm quite good."

"Shorthand?"

"I think I'm rather good."

"Did Mr. Campbell pick you out because of your ability or because of your figure?"

Susan Fisher laughed in an embarrassed manner.

"Go ahead," Miss Corning said, "answer the question."

"Frankly, Miss Corning, I think he picked me out because of my figure. But after he had tried out my shorthand and typing, I think he kept me because of my ability."

"Ever make passes at you?"

Susan hesitated, then said, quietly, "Yes."

"Ever get anywhere?"

"No."

"What kind of passes?"

"Just the ordinary kind, just sort of exploring to see where the "No Trespassing' signs were."

"Can't blame him for that," Miss Corning said. "Any normal man will do that with a good-looking girl who's working with him. All right now, is Mr. Campbell crooked or not?"

"I'm sure I couldn't tell you."

"What do you think?"

"I don't know, Miss Corning, and I wish I did. There are some things going on there that bother me very much. I'm not in the auditing department. I simply type up statements and—"

"You run an adding machine?"

"Oh, yes."

"All right, go on. You type up statements and then what?"

"Well, I get the statements primarily from the auditing department or Mr. Campbell gives me the statements. . . . I will say this, the business is so departmentalized that, frankly, I doubt if anyone other than Mr. Campbell has a general comprehensive picture of what goes on. And I've been concerned about this Mojave Monarch Mine."

"Why?"

"Well, for one thing," Susan said, "I went out there to Mojave on a drive. I didn't have any idea of looking at the mine; in fact, I'd forgotten all about the mine being in that part of the country. I was just out there driving around and I saw a sign on a road, a rather weather-beaten piece of wood nailed to a stake. It said on this sign, 'Mojave Monarch.' So I turned in there just out of curiosity."

"And what did you find?"

"I found a mine, but there certainly was no one working there. I went to one of the service stations and asked if there was any other Mojave Monarch around there and the service station man said he'd never heard of any, that the only Mojave Monarch he knew had been closed ever since one of the veins had faulted out."

"The monthly reports show that the mine is operating, but operating at a heavy loss," Miss Corning said.

"I'm quite familiar with the monthly reports," Susan Fisher said. "I do the typing."

"But you don't think the mine is working?"

"I don't know."

"Then if the reports are false, Mr. Campbell is crooked?"

"I wouldn't say that. The reports come in from a manager in Mojave and—"

"Endicott Campbell has never been out to Mojave to look the mine over?"

"I don't know."

"Well, if he's going to manage my business he should know what's going on in a mine that's almost in his back yard."

Susan Fisher said nothing.

"Well," Miss Corning snapped, "say something! Should he or shouldn't he?"

Susan said, "Mr. Campbell is very, very busy around the office. He's making out reports and correlating affairs and he's had quite a bit of trouble with the income-tax people. Frankly, I don't think he's ever gone to Mojave. I think he feels the mine is somewhat out of his jurisdiction. I don't know where he—"

The door opened and Endicott Campbell, standing in the doorway, said, "Who says I've never gone to Mojave? What's going on here? What are you folks trying to do, get behind my back and tear my business reputation to shreds?"

"I suppose," Miss Corning said, "that irate, rasping voice belongs to my manager, Endicott Campbell. Come in, Mr. Campbell, and sit down. It's customary to knock before entering."

"I don't care whether it's customary or not," Campbell said. "I don't know what's going on here, and, despite the fact that I'm working for you, Miss Corning, I resent the idea of you coming here and gathering my employees around you to discuss the efficiency of my management before you have even taken the matter up with me or let me know that you were here."

"Now just a minute, Campbell," Mason said. "We tried to get in touch with you on the telephone."

"How did *you* know Miss Corning was here?" Campbell demanded.

"I anticipated her arrival," Mason said.

"She wasn't due until tomorrow."

"I know she wasn't," Mason told him, "but in case you want to know, I had men watching the airport so that we could pick her up on her arrival. That was something that you *could* have done if you'd wanted to—or if you'd thought of it."

"I'm afraid my mind doesn't work in these somewhat devious channels," Campbell said. And then to Miss Corning, "I'm sorry,

Miss Corning, that I'm acting in this manner, but, frankly, I'm angry."

"Go ahead, go ahead," Miss Corning said. "Get angry. I like to hear two men fight."

"Well, I don't like the idea of Mr. Mason horning in on this thing and trying to get around behind my back."

"Now, just a minute," Mason told him. "In the first place, I don't give a damn whether you like it or not. In the second place, nobody is going behind your back. We're out in front of you and scooping up the ball that you'd fumbled. Now, just remember one thing. I'm representing Susan Fisher. She's my client. I have an idea that you're intending to make her some sort of a football that you can kick around in order to disguise your own shortcomings. I don't intend to let you do it. I wanted Miss Corning to know the facts as they were before you had a chance to garble them."

"Well," Campbell said, "I would have liked to have had Miss Corning know the facts as they were before *you* got to her and garbled them."

"We're talking facts," Mason said.

"You were talking about the intimate affairs of the company."

"We were answering Miss Corning's questions about the Mojave Monarch, and I think that perhaps Miss Corning can well ask *you* about the Mojave Monarch. If you think we've garbled the facts, I'd like to hear what you have to say about them."

"And so would I," Miss Corning said.

Much of the belligerence left Campbell's manner. "All right," he said, "as far as the Mojave Monarch is concerned, the only thing I can say to Miss Corning is that apparently I was victimized by a man who was in charge of the property at Mojave, a man who apparently made false reports to me in person, in writing, and over the telephone."

"Have you ever been out there?" Miss Corning demanded.

"I've been out there," Campbell said. "I've just returned from there. I was out there yesterday. I'm not a mining man, Miss Corning. I'm an executive. I specialize in the supervision of real-estate investments. The mine activities were entirely out of my line. I told you that when you hired me.

"As far as the real-estate activities are concerned, you'll find that you have made a tidy profit under my management. As far as the Mojave Monarch is concerned, I've been victimized and you have incurred a very substantial loss because of that. I'm sorry, but I was so busy with real estate that I had to delegate the mining activities to the manager, Ken Lowry. The mine was in a field about which I knew virtually nothing.

"The profits on the real estate which I have handled for you have been *very* substantial, and have more than offset any losses on the Mojave Monarch. I would like to discuss that matter with you in detail and not in front of an audience.

"And as far as this young woman is concerned, this woman who was so anxious to get to your ears before I had an opportunity to say anything, I am very much afraid the books show that she has embezzled something over a hundred and sixty-one thousand dollars in cash. I have had the auditing department working all night and a very serious cash shortage has shown up. It shows a devilish ingenuity, as well as quite a familiarity with the affairs of the company."

"All right," Mason said, "now it comes out in the open. You're accusing Susan Fisher of embezzling money from the corporation?"

"I'm not making any accusations at the present time. I'm simply reporting confidentially to my employer what the auditing department has uncovered as a result of all-night activity."

"You consider yourself blameless in the matter?" Mason asked.

"Certainly."

"You're the executive manager of the business, you think that you have been working efficiently and yet it is only within the last twenty-four hours you have found out there is a shortage of something over a hundred and sixty thousand dollars in the company, and that the Mojave Monarch has been operated in such a way that Miss Corning has been swindled out of many thousands of dollars?"

"I don't have to answer those questions. I don't like the way you phrase them and I don't have to submit to cross-examination by you," Campbell said. "For your information, my business management has netted something over three-quarters of a million dollars for Miss Corning. A man can't make profits in a business of that magnitude without having some areas of the business which are not given his undivided personal attention."

"And in these areas of the business which have not been given your undivided personal attention, there have been shortages and swindles?" Mason asked.

"I've told you I don't have to submit to your cross-examination."

Mason said, "You accuse my client of embezzling and you'll be submitting to my cross-examination, either here or in court."

"By the time we get to court," Campbell said, "I'll have the facts and figures so well established that even you can't alibi your client into the clear."

Mason said, "For your information, Miss Corning, Mr. Campbell evidently kept a shoe box in his closet. This shoe box was crammed full of one-hundred-dollar bills. His seven-year-old son inadvertently picked up this shoe box and—"

"And for your information, Miss Corning," Campbell interrupted, his voice raised in anger, "that's a dastardly lie!"

"We can prove what I'm saying," Mason said.

"Only by the unsubstantiated word of your client," Campbell charged. "That shoe box full of hundred-dollar bills was never seen by anybody except Susan Fisher."

Susan said, "Your son brought the box in, Mr. Campbell. Where's Carleton now?"

Endicott Campbell said, "Get this thing straight once and for all, all of you. My son is not going to be dragged into this. I am not going to have his emotions twisted and distorted against his father. We're going to leave my son out of this. He is not going to be interrogated by anyone."

"I take it," Mason said, "by that you mean you have taken steps to see that he can't be found."

"I am acting in accordance with my conscientious convictions as his father. I am performing my duties as a parent."

"In other words," Mason said, "after we strip your speech of all its high-sounding talk about your duties as a parent, it comes down to the fact that Susan Fisher says your son gave her a shoe box belonging to you and that this shoe box was full of hundred-dollar bills. You say that that is a complete lie, that no one has seen the shoe box except Susan Fisher, and in order to establish your point you have put your son somewhere in hiding so that he can't be interrogated."

"You are a lawyer," Campbell said. "You can twist things around to suit your own purpose. I made the statement which I think Miss Corning will accept at face value."

"All right," Amelia Corning said, "I think I've heard enough to get a pretty good picture of the situation. I've given you and your client a chance to talk, Mr. Mason, and now I'm going to give Mr. Campbell a chance to talk."

"I will say this," Endicott Campbell said, "I tried to humor my son yesterday morning. He had a shoe box which contained some of his treasures. I had a shoe box containing some dress shoes. I made some joking remark about a trade. He evidently took the shoe box containing the patent-leather shoes. He told me that he gave that shoe box to Susan Fisher. He said she put it in the safe, that he didn't get it back. That is the complete story of the shoe box. *I* know what was in that shoe box. It was a pair of dress shoes. I can show you the sales slip where they were purchased. Now if Miss Fisher will kindly produce the shoe box she claims was filled with money we'll see what's in it."

Amelia Corning said, "The situation is quite clear. Somebody is lying. Now if you folks will retire I'll sit down and talk things over with Mr. Campbell. I take it, Mr. Campbell, you feel that you're able to substantiate some of the charges you've made?"

"Unfortunately," Campbell said, "Sue Fisher has disposed of much of the documentary evidence. She *says* she turned it over to a woman who arrived here yesterday and impersonated you. If Miss Fisher had simply refrained from doing all of these things until I could have been given an opportunity as manager of the business to okay what she was doing, I feel that we would—"

"I tried and tried to get you," Sue interrupted.

"Well, you didn't try hard enough or in the right place," Campbell said. "For your information I canceled a golf game in order to make a hurried trip to Mojave to check up on what was being done at that mine. You took it on yourself to turn over confidential company records to a perfect stranger. This is all very, very convenient for you, Miss Fisher. For my part, I think this impersonator was someone you dug up in a last-minute effort to so confuse the issues that you couldn't be convicted of the embezzlement."

"All right," Mason said, "you've made that as an accusation. Now let me ask you this, Mr. Campbell. Is there any reason why *any* person who was responsible for the embezzlement, whether it was Susan Fisher, John Doe or Endicott Campbell, couldn't have very cleverly arranged this entire impersonation so that the documentary evidence of the embezzlement would disappear and the money would also disappear?"

Campbell smiled frostily. "So that's going to be the angle you use in your defense; a counter-offensive, eh? Well, I'll meet you on those grounds, Mr. Perry Mason, at the proper time and in the proper place. And right now I'm going to make a confidential report to my employer and believe me, it's going to be confidential.

"You call up Miss Corning in an hour and you'll find out your client wasn't as smart as she thought she was. I've managed to get enough evidence in my hands to establish her duplicity."

Miss Corning said, "You folks have all had a chance to let off steam. I've heard Susan Fisher's side of the case. Now I'll hear yours, Mr. Campbell. The rest of you, clear out!"

Chapter Five

Out in the corridor Mason, Della Street and Susan Fisher walked slowly toward the elevator.

Midway to the elevator Sue Fisher said, "Mr. Mason, can't we do something to find Carleton? He's had that English governess of his take the boy and go somewhere."

Mason said nothing until they had reached the elevator and the lawyer had punched the button. "The boy," he said, "didn't know what was in the shoe box, did he?"

"No, he just knew it was Daddy's treasure."

"And his daddy," Mason said, "insists the treasure was a pair of dress shoes. So that isn't going to help us very much. . . . Even if we recover the shoe box full of money you can't prove anything, because Endicott Campbell will swear that there was a pair of dress shoes in it when he let his son take the box. He can't help it if you threw the dress shoes into the trash and filled the box full of hundred-dollar bills, the result of your embezzlement."

Sue Fisher looked at him in dismay as the full significance of the situation dawned upon her. "Well," she asked, "what *can* we do?"

"That," Mason said, "will depend very largely upon certain developments in the situation and on what kind of woman Miss Corning is."

"She looks to me like someone who would be hard to fool," Susan Fisher said.

"In that case," Mason pointed out, "Endicott Campbell is probably having a handful of problems right now."

"So we wait for something to—to turn up?"

Mason gave her one of his warm smiles. "You do, Sue," he said, "but we are going to take steps which will encourage things to turn up. —There's a saying in the newspaper business that a good reporter makes his own luck and I think we are going out to make some luck."

"Where?"

"Oh, various places."

"Mojave?" she asked.

"I wouldn't be too surprised," Mason said.

"Oh, Mr. Mason, can I go with you, please? Can I . . . ?"

The lawyer shook his head. "We don't want you to do anything which could even be remotely considered as flight or avoiding questioning. You go right to your apartment and stay there. Stay by the telephone. If anything out of the ordinary happens, telephone Paul Drake at once."

The elevator cage slid into position and the door glided open.

Mason patted her shoulder. "Remember," he said, "that we're playing a game and we've got to play our cards just right . . . just—exactly—*right*."

Chapter Six

Sunday traffic made for delays in the first part of the drive. Mason, his face granite hard, said little.

Then as the traffic began to thin out, the lawyer put the car into speed.

Knowing Mason's feelings about safe driving and his conviction that an automobile driven at high speed was a deadly missile which should be operated only by one who was in full possession of his faculties and concentrating on the driving, Della Street made no effort to discuss the case until after they came up over the little hill, crossed the railroad tracks and saw the town of Mojave spread out along the main street.

The desert air was crystal clear. The buildings seemed etched in the afternoon sunlight.

Mason pulled in to a filling station, said to the attendant, "Fill it up," then after the hose had been placed in the tank, Mason said casually, "Do you happen to know a man named Lowry? Ken Lowry?"

"Sure," the attendant said. "He's— There he is, right across the street, getting in that pickup!"

Mason followed the direction of the other man's pointing finger and saw a somewhat battered pickup with the name MOJAVE MONARCH MINE on the side door.

The lawyer started hurrying across the street but Lowry pulled out when Mason was still halfway to the car.

The attendant at the service station gave a shrill whistle and the man at the wheel of the pickup jerked his head, saw Mason waving at him, and slowed the car to a stop.

Mason approached the car. "You're Lowry of the Mojave Monarch?"

"Right."

"I'm Perry Mason, an attorney from Los Angeles, and I'd like very much to talk with you."

"What about?"

"About the mining business."

Lowry smiled and shook his head. "I don't talk business with strangers," he said. "Leastwise, not mining business."

"All right," Mason said, "if you don't talk, will you listen?"

Della Street, hurrying across the road, came up to the car.

Mason said, "This is my secretary, Miss Street, Mr. Lowry."

Lowry, a grizzled, leathery-faced, gray-eyed individual in the early forties, surveyed Della appreciatively. A gust of desert wind whipped her skirts and Lowry promptly lowered his eyes to take in the scenery. "How do you do, ma'am? Very pleased to meet you," he said.

Della Street gave him her most winning smile and her hand. "How do you do, Mr. Lowry?"

"I know you're busy," Mason said, "but we drove out here just to see you. Could we have a few minutes of your time?"

"I can't talk."

"Will you give us a few minutes?"

"I'll listen for a few minutes."

"Where can we talk?" Mason asked.

"Right here's as good a place as any," Lowry said.

Della caught Mason's eye, said, "Why can't we get in the car with Mr. Lowry and talk there? That way we won't attract so much attention and won't have to raise our voices."

Lowry hesitated and Mason said, "Good idea, Della."

The lawyer walked around the front of the automobile, held the door open for Della Street.

Della jumped in with a quick flash of generously displayed nylon which, for the moment, held Lowry's undivided attention. Then Mason got in beside her and closed the door.

"I'm listening," Lowry said.

He swung halfway around in the seat so that he could be facing Perry Mason and as he caught the full dazzling effect of Della Street's eyes he settled back against the cushion, slid his right arm along the back of the seat and indicated by his manner that despite his words he wasn't going to be in too great a hurry to terminate the interview.

"I suppose Endicott Campbell has been here and warned you against talking to anyone," Mason said.

Lowry merely grinned.

"And perhaps he even mentioned my name," Mason went on.

Lowry said, "I'm listening."

"All right," Mason told him, "I'm talking. I'd like to know something about the Mojave Monarch Mine. I'd like to know how the thing is set up, how it operated, how long the mine's been shut down."

Lowry sat silent.

"Well?" Mason asked.

"Not talking," Lowry said. "What's more, I'm not going to talk."

Della Street said, "Mr. Lowry, would you listen to me?"

"I'm listening."

Della Street said, "A young woman, a most attractive young woman, is being charged with a crime. Mr. Mason is trying to represent her. He isn't doing this for money. She hasn't paid him as much as a nickel. She can't afford to pay him even a fraction of what his services are worth. She's a young secretary who has her whole life in front of her. That life can be ruined if the facts are distorted. We're trying to get the true facts, that's all we want. There's no reason why anyone should be afraid of the truth, is there, Mr. Lowry? . . . Or *is* there any reason for being afraid of the truth?"

"Not as far as I'm concerned."

"Then why aren't you willing to answer a few simple questions so that we can get the real facts? Do you have any idea what it means to a woman to go to prison? A woman only has a few of the golden years in her life when she's attractive. Even at the best, when she can get lots of vitamins, fresh air, sunshine, exercise and mental stimulation she begins to fade after a few years.

"Think of what it means to a young, attractive woman to have the prison doors close on her and to realize that as she endures that treadmill existence her beauty is slipping through her fingers."

Lowry said, "There hasn't any beauty slipped through *your* fingers, ma'am, if you don't mind my saying so."

Della Street gave him her most dazzling smile. "I don't mind your saying so," she said, "but it seems to me you're a fair man, you're a square shooter, you're the type of individual who scorns subterfuge and deceit. Now it's my best guess that you've had to do things that you didn't want to do and that has worried you. In fact, I think you're worried right now. —Mr. Mason is a very clever lawyer. There's just a chance he could help you."

"I don't need any help," Lowry said.

"Perhaps you think you don't, but there are all sorts of angles to a thing like this," Della Street went on. "Remember that Endicott Campbell is very much interested in saving his own skin."

Lowry looked across at Perry Mason and said, "She's a pretty darn good saleswoman."

"Convincing you?" Mason asked, smiling.

"Not yet."

"She should have convinced you by this time," Mason told him, "because she's telling the truth."

"She sure makes it *sound* convincing."

"The truth is always convincing," Della Street said. "There's something unmistakable about the truth. Now I'm going to risk getting thrown out of here right on the sidewalk by telling you that you've got yourself to think of. You're an outdoor man, I can tell that by looking at you. You're accustomed to the big spaces, you're accustomed to wind on your face, you're accustomed to sunlight, you're accustomed to lots of fresh air. Don't think for a minute that you're completely in the clear in this thing, Mr. Lowry.

"I've told you what it would mean to a young woman to go to prison but do you realize what it means to an outdoor man to go to prison, to be shut up within stones walls, to be deprived of sunlight, of air, of freedom? Do you realize how many people of that sort contract prison tuberculosis?"

Lowry's face flushed. "Say," he said angrily, "what are you doing? Threatening me?"

Della Street looked him straight in the eyes and said, *"I'm* not threatening you, Mr. Lowry, *I'm* warning you. You're a pretty good specimen of manhood. I wouldn't like to see you spend the next ten years behind bars. I'm also going to tell you something else. My boss, Mr. Mason, is a pretty smart individual. If you tell him your story perhaps he can help you."

Lowry doggedly shook his head.

Della Street whirled to Mason, lowered her right eye in a wink, said, "All right, Chief, let's go."

"Now wait a minute," Lowry said. "I'm thinking things over a little bit."

"You'd better think fast then," Mason said, following up Della Street's lead.

There was silence for several seconds, then Lowry again shook his head. "Nope," he said, "I'm not talking."

"All right," Mason said to Della Street, "get your notebook, Della."

Della Street took a notebook out of her purse.

"Put down the date and the time," Mason said, "and take this statement: This is dictated in the presence of Ken Lowry, Manager of the Mojave Monarch. We called on Mr. Lowry and asked him to tell us something about the operation of the mine. We pointed out to him that a young woman was being charged with crime, that she was innocent; that circumstances had conspired against her and that she was quite possibly the victim of a frame-up. Mr. Lowry would make absolutely no statement. He wouldn't tell us anything about the operation of the mine, he wouldn't divulge the location of the mine, he wouldn't tell us how long it had been shut down; he refused to discuss anything, thereby indicating his own bias and that he was trying to cover up the true facts."

"Now wait a minute," Lowry said. "Since you're writing that down you just put in there that I said I'm not covering up anything, that I've simply been instructed not to discuss the matter with anyone and particularly with Perry Mason."

"Who gave you those instructions?" Mason asked.

"Endicott Campbell, if you want to know."

"All right," Mason said grimly, "before I get done with Endicott Campbell he may not be giving anyone instructions. And if you want to tie in with him, go ahead. But before you plunge along in blind loyalty to Campbell you'd better find out something about what Campbell has been doing and find out what the facts are.

"I'll probably be cross-examining you in court, Mr. Lowry. Don't say that I didn't give you every opportunity."

Mason opened the door of the car.

Lowry said angrily, "All right, you've given me every opportunity. I don't have to talk to you and I'm not going to."

Della Street turned to him, put her hand impulsively on his arm. "Listen, Mr. Lowry," she said, "please let's not misunderstand each other."

"I'm not misunderstanding anybody."

"Perhaps *we're* misunderstanding *you*. But let me put it to you this way. You've had an opportunity to see Endicott Campbell. You've known him for some time and—"

"Yesterday was the first time I ever set eyes on him," Lowry said.

"All right," Della Street went on, glancing significantly at Perry Mason. "You probably pride yourself on judging character. How do you judge Endicott Campbell? Would you go out on a prospecting trip with him? Would you like to have him as a partner?"

"I pick my own partners," Lowry said, "and I pick 'em carefully."

"No, you don't," Della Street said. "Endicott Campbell picked you as a partner and he's sold you a bill of goods. You're his partner in this thing right now, just the same as though you were partners in a mining enterprise."

"He isn't any partner of mine," Lowry said.

"That's what you think," Mason said. "Campbell came out here. He handed you a razzle-dazzle and told you not to talk and now you're refusing to give out pertinent information—information that we're entitled to, information that you should give out in order to protect yourself, to say nothing of this young woman."

"Now wait a minute, wait a minute," Lowry said. "This thing sort of gets me when you put it that way. I tell you, the guy isn't my partner."

"And I tell you he is," Mason said. "He's hypnotized you into a partnership. You're playing right along with him. You're following his instructions and doing exactly what he's told you to do. You're not his partner in a mine, you're his partner in something that may be a criminal enterprise and the partnership may leave you in a lot of trouble."

For the first time Lowry turned, took his eyes off his visitors, looked out through the windshield, down the long street.

"Why should I tell you anything?" he asked.

"Why shouldn't you?" Mason said. "Unless you have something to conceal. —I'll put it another way. Why should you go into partnership with Campbell just because he comes out and tells you what he wants you to do?"

"Because in a way I'm working for Campbell."

"Following Campbell's instructions?"

"Well, following instructions from headquarters."

"And do you think Endicott Campbell is representing headquarters?"

"He said he was."

Mason's smile was enigmatic.

Lowry narrowed his eyes, took a deep breath. "All right," he said, "I *want* to talk. I want to explain my position in this matter. But I promised Campbell I'd not tell you anything."

"Then you did take Campbell as a partner," Della Street said.

"For heaven's sake, quit harping on that," Lowry said irritably. "I tell you, the man isn't my partner."

Mason looked at Della Street, smiled and shook his head tolerantly.

Della Street said, "I'm sorry you can't see it, Mr. Lowry."

Lowry thought things over for a moment, then said, "All right, I'm going to tell you this much. I did some peculiar things but everything I did was the result of orders I received directly from Miss Corning."

"Personally?" Mason asked.

"Over the long-distance telephone."

"How many conversations?"

"Two."

"From South America?"

"No. She called me up from Miami. She made two business trips up to the States and she called me personally."

"You know her personally?" Mason asked.

"I've never met her."

"In other words," Mason said, "you listened to a voice on the telephone. The voice on the telephone told you to do certain things. Those things were highly irregular. Then a man whom you've never seen before comes out here and tells you not to discuss those things. . . . It seems to me you're rather a credulous individual, Mr. Lowry."

"You mean that wasn't Amelia Corning who was talking with me on the telephone?"

"I don't know," Mason said. "Furthermore, you don't know. Let me ask you this: did Endicott Campbell tell you that a woman showed up yesterday who impersonated Amelia Corning?"

"Heavens, no!" Lowry said.

"Well, she did. If anyone is desperate enough to impersonate Amelia Corning in a personal interview, it certainly wouldn't be hard to do it over long-distance telephone."

Lowry thought things over.

"All right," he said at length. "I'm not going to buy Endicott Campbell as my partner. I don't like the guy. He's a little too smooth and a little too slick. I guess you opened my eyes, Miss Street, when you asked me if I'd like to camp out in the desert with him. I wouldn't share blankets with that guy on a bet. I don't think I'd trust him."

Mason said, "Now is a good time to get the situation clarified."

"I'll tell you this much," Lowry said. "I was hired by a letter from Amelia Corning. She had taken over the Mojave Monarch. She'd bought all the mine—lock, stock and barrel. She told me to go ahead and run it in accordance with her instructions."

"What about the Corning Mining, Smelting and Investment Company?"

"That's an affiliated enterprise," Lowry said, "but I was working directly under Miss Corning and I was making reports to her. . . . Well, we ran into trouble. The vein faulted on us and I didn't know what to do. I wrote to her and she told me that she'd let the Los Angeles company give me instructions. Then the next day she called me up and said she'd changed her mind. She asked me what I thought about closing the mine up and I told her that I thought it was the only thing to do; that we might spend a fortune trying to find that vein.

"All right, she told me she'd let me know. Then she called me up a little later and told me that for tax purposes she couldn't afford to have the mine closed. She told me she'd turned the thing over to the Corning Mining, Smelting and Investment Company with headquarters in Los Angeles; that I would write every month and send them figures on what the payroll would have been if the mine was going full blast; that as far as the books were concerned I'd be having twelve men on each of three eight-hour shifts working here, which would make a total of thirty-six employees. I was to tell the Los Angeles office how much money I wanted for this payroll, and they'd send me a check which I was to cash in one-hundred-dollar bills, deduct my salary, and then mail those hundred-dollar bills in to Los Angeles. In that way, she said, it was just a cash transaction and all she'd be out would be the employer's liability insurance and incidental expenses, but as far as the books were concerned, for tax purposes it would show that the mine was still being operated. . . . Now then, was that crooked?"

"What do you think?" Mason asked.

"That's what bothers me," Lowry said. "I followed instructions all right and did what she told me but I didn't like doing it."

"All right," Mason said, "you sent the money to the Los Angeles company?"

"No. I sent the money to the Corning Affiliated Enterprises in Los Angeles. I sent it to a post office box there."

"You sent it in the form of cash?"

"I just got that check cashed at the bank here in hundred-dollar bills. I'd deduct the amount of my salary, then wrap the rest of those hundred-dollar bills in a plain package. Now that's the thing that I didn't like about the whole business. She told me not to register the money, not to have it appear that there was anything of value in the shipment; to just wrap it up and send it parcel post to this Corning Affiliated Enterprises at the post office box.

"I'd get checks from the Corning Mining, Smelting and Investment Company to cover all operating expenses. Every two weeks I'd endorse the check and take it in to the bank here to be cashed."

"Didn't the bank know something was wrong?" Mason asked.

"What do you mean wrong?"

"Well, I mean, didn't the bank think there was something unusual?"

"Sure the bank thought there was something unusual, but the bank wasn't blowing the whistle. I told the bank that I was acting under direct orders from headquarters and . . . Well, the bank knows me."

"You've lived here quite a while?"

"That's right."

"And, I take it, have a pretty good local reputation for integrity?"

"I certainly hope so."

"How much money did you send altogether to Los Angeles?"

"Somewhere around a hundred and eighty-one thousand dollars."

"You sent in money for social security and . . ."

"No, I just sent the cash back to Los Angeles."

"Did you ever get any receipt or anything?"

"I never got so much as the scratch of a pen from the Corning Affiliated Enterprises, but I'd receive a telephone call after each shipment telling me that the shipment had been received okay."

"Who made the call?"

"I don't know who it was. Some woman. She'd simply state this was the Corning Affiliated Enterprises office and that she wanted to report the shipment had been received okay and to keep on as before."

"Then you've heard two voices over the telephone," Mason said, "the voice of the woman who acknowledged the shipments, and the voice of the woman who told you she was Amelia Corning."

"Well, I guess so," Lowry said. "I don't remember the Corning voice too well."

"Could it have been the same voice?"

"I don't know. I—I—I'm beginning to get bothered about all this, Mr. Mason."

"How about the voice that reported the receipt of shipments to you over the telephone? Do you think you could recognize that voice if you heard it?"

"I have an idea I could. At least I could make a stab at it."

"Where were those calls received?"

"At my house at the mine, the manager's house."

"During office hours?"

"No. Every one of them would come in in the evening."

"And Endicott Campbell told you not to say anything about this to anyone?"

"He told me not to say anything to you, but the more you come to think of it the more you realize that I'm in a peculiar position here. I'm not buying Endicott Campbell as a partner."

"That's right," Mason told him. "I think you'll realize that you did the right thing by telling me what happened."

"Well," Lowry said, "the thing that got me was what Miss Street said about having Campbell as my partner."

"That's right," Mason told him, "you don't want him as your partner. . . . Now then, have you heard anything from Amelia Corning lately?"

"Not a word."

"Did you make any other reports on what you were doing?"

"No, I was told not to—just to cash the check and send the money to Los Angeles."

"Didn't that impress you as being a peculiar way of running a business?"

"Sure it did. But I figured that there was a tax angle in it somewhere and, of course, you hate to have a mine close down. It gives it a black eye. Of course, people around here know the mine's closed but as far as the books of the mining company are concerned, it would send out a big payroll every month and every month it would get back a shipment, which I suppose they'd claim came from ore. Since it was in the form of cash it couldn't be traced."

"That's your supposition," Mason said.

"That's right."

"And, as you so aptly remarked, since it's in the form of cash it couldn't be traced."

"Say, what are you getting at?" Lowry asked.

Mason opened the car door, said, "Just be careful who you pick as a partner, Lowry. Perhaps truth is the best partner you can pick."

Abruptly Lowry reached out and shook hands. "Say," he said, "I'm awfully glad I met you, and this secretary of yours. I think you've given me some pretty darn good advice. I'm feeling a lot better right now than I have been feeling all day."

Della Street gave him a smile and her hand. "It's been so nice meeting you, Mr. Lowry," she said. "I could see that you were uncomfortable keeping this stuff bottled up inside of you. You're not the type of individual to get mixed up in any shady transaction."

"This thing's been worrying me for a long while," Lowry admitted.

"Thanks a lot," Mason told him. "It was awfully nice meeting you."

Lowry watched Mason and Della Street as they walked back to the service station.

"Thanks, Della," Mason said, "you pulled that one out of the fire very nicely. That was good psychology, telling him that he'd bought Endicott Campbell as a partner. . . . How did you think of that approach?"

"I'm darned if I know, Chief," Della Street said. "It just popped into my head since he was the outdoor, mining type."

"I think I need your head along with me all the time," Mason told her.

"It's a good idea," Della Street said. "It's available. What do we do now?"

"Now," Mason said, "we beat it back to Los Angeles. But first we get Paul Drake on the telephone. We concentrate on Endicott Campbell. We also find out all we can about this Corning Affiliated Enterprises. —And I'm afraid we're not going to find out very much."

Chapter Seven

From a telephone booth at Lancaster, Mason called Paul Drake.

"Put a tail on Endicott Campbell," Mason instructed. "This thing is even bigger than I thought it was, Paul, and somehow I have a feeling it's deadly dangerous. Get a tail on Campbell and try and find out where that son of his is."

Drake said, "That's going to be a pretty difficult assignment. He anticipated you'd be looking for the boy and he planned the cover-up well in advance. When an intelligent man does that, he makes it almost impossible for any private agency to backtrack him. The police might be able to, but it will be a long and expensive job if we do it."

"See what you can do anyway," Mason said. "I'm on my way back to the city. Wait in the office for me. I want to see you when I arrive."

"What did you do up there—any good?"

"I think so," Mason said.

"Let's hope so," Drake told him, "because you're sure as hell running up a detective bill, Perry."

"My credit still good?" Mason asked.

"Up to a million," Drake told him.

"All right. Keep going," Mason said, and hung up.

He called the number of the Arthenium Hotel so that no one except the exchange operator would know it was a long-distance call and asked to be connected with Amelia Corning's suite.

When he heard her voice on the line, Mason said, "This is Perry Mason, Miss Corning. I'd like to see you some time in the early part of the evening."

"Oh, that will be wonderful, Mr. Mason. I enjoyed talking with you and I think you and that client of yours can do me quite a bit of good. For your information, my talk with Endicott Campbell was not in the least satisfactory."

"I see," Mason said noncommittally.

"Now, I've just received a wire that my sister and my Brazilian agent have left Miami and are due to arrive here on the ten twenty-five plane. I'd like to see you before they arrive . . . could you run up now? . . . Where are you?"

"It would be inconvenient for me to come up right now," Mason said, without divulging his location, "but how would seven thirty do?"

"I'd like to see you before that but I realize, of course, that you're a very busy man. I'm going to do something rather nice for that Susan Fisher. I have come to the conclusion that . . . well, I'd better tell you that personally when I see you. And you'll bring your secretary with you?"

"Yes, indeed," Mason said.

"Well, just come right up. Don't bother to be announced. I'll be expecting you at seven thirty."

"At seventy thirty," Mason said.

"There's one thing perhaps I should tell you, Mr. Mason. I'm a demon for being prompt. If you can be here at seven thirty we'll fix that time. If there's any question about it, we'll make it seven forty-five."

"Seven thirty will be all right," Mason told her. "I'll be there."

"Thank you, Mr. Mason. Good-by."

Mason returned to the car, said to Della Street, "We have a date at seven thirty on the button with Amelia Corning. Paul is putting a tail on Endicott Campbell."

"How did Endicott Campbell get along with Amelia Corning? Any clues?" she asked.

"More than clues," Mason told her. "Miss Corning didn't make any bones about it. She said the interview was highly unsatisfactory."

Della Street grinned. "I just had a feeling that fellow was going to overreach himself."

"He can still make trouble," Mason said. "We're going to have to move right along, Della, and Miss Corning emphasized particularly that she wanted her appointments kept on the dot. By the way, her sister and her business agent have flown up from South America. They wired her from Miami and they're coming in on the ten twenty-five plane."

"Then the net is closing around Endicott Campbell," Della Street said.

"It could be closing," Mason said. "But don't ever discount a man of that type. He's ingenious, clever, daring, and he very probably has been anticipating a situation of this sort for some time and has planned ahead."

"But what good do his plans do him?" Della said. "Sure, he had his getaway money all neatly tucked into a shoe box and then his son took it and gave it to Susan Fisher."

"And then what happened to it?" Mason asked.

"Well," Della Street said, "either the person who was impersonating Amelia Corning got it, or . . ."

"Go ahead," Mason said, as she paused.

"Or," she said, "Endicott Campbell went back to the safe and got it. . . . Of course he did, Chief."

"He had the opportunity," Mason said, "and undoubtedly he went back to the office and opened the safe. But remember, if the woman impersonating Miss Corning had taken the box, it wasn't there by the time Campbell arrived."

"But, Chief, I don't see what difference it makes. They were working hand in glove. He deliberately planted this imposter and set the stage so that Susan Fisher would fall for it. She gave this woman all of the documentary proof that would indicate irregularities and—"

"That, of course," Mason interposed, "was the reason she was sent up there. But a shoe box full of hundred-dollar bills is something different."

"You mean she may have double-crossed Campbell?"

Mason said, "Campbell is acting in a most peculiar way. You know, there's just a possibility, Della, that someone double-crossed him and he doesn't know for sure whether it was Susan Fisher who got the money and secreted it after telling him the story about leaving the shoe box in the safe, or whether his accomplice, the woman he got to pose as Amelia Corning, decided she might just as well look at the side of the bread that had the butter."

"In other words, you feel, from the way he's acting, that he doesn't have the money?" Della Street asked.

"It's a possibility," Mason said. "Let's let it go at that."

Mason eased the car up to the legal limit of speed and concentrated on his driving.

As they neared Los Angeles, Della Street consulted her wrist watch several times, glanced apprehensively at Mason. "Are you going to try to call on Paul Drake first?" she asked.

"We won't have time," Mason said. "The road was a little slower than I thought it would be and we're going to have to go right to the Arthenium in order to keep our appointment."

"Do you want me to drop you off there and then go to check with Paul and have him call you?"

"No," Mason said. "I want you to go up with me. Incidentally, Miss Corning asked for you particularly. She wanted me to be sure and bring you along. You've evidently made quite an impression with her . . . in fact, Della, you've been invaluable today."

"You make me blush," she said demurely.

"And you make me very, very proud," Mason said. "You really did a job working out that approach with Lowry. I think we have some information now that will prove of the greatest interest to Amelia Corning. I wouldn't be too surprised if she didn't want to swear out a warrant for Campbell's arrest. There is, however, one thing that bothers me."

"What's that?"

"I think Campbell must realize that we dashed out to Mojave to look up that mine."

"Well?" she asked.

"In that event," Mason said, "he'll wonder what we've found out."

"Does that make any difference?" she asked.

"It makes this difference," Mason told her. "If he wanted to find out just how much we had discovered, what would he do?"

"Why, he'd . . . I guess he'd call Lowry."

"Exactly," Mason said. "And when Lowry talks with him on the telephone now, Lowry isn't going to be the same co-operative conspirator that he was earlier in the day. So Campbell is going to ask him if he told us the story of what had happened, and Lowry would make a poor liar."

"He wouldn't even try to lie," Della Street said. "He'd tell the truth."

Mason nodded. "So then try thinking what a desperate Endicott Campbell would be doing all this time before we can get back."

Della Street became thoughtful. "That isn't a reassuring thought."

Mason nodded, gave the Sunday-evening traffic his frowning concentration, arrived in front of the Arthenium Hotel at seven twenty-seven.

Mason handed the doorman a couple of dollars. "You've got to take care of that car for me," he said. "I haven't time to park it."

"I'll take care of it. It'll be all right, right there for a while," the doorman said. "Will you be long?"

"I don't think so. We'll let you know if we're detained beyond ten or fifteen minutes."

Mason and Della Street hurried across the lobby to the elevators, then up to the Presidential Suite.

As Mason and Della Street walked down the corridor toward the Presidential Suite, Della Street said, "It looks as if the door is open."

Mason observed the oblong of bright light which was coming from the door of the suite and quickened his pace.

The door of the Presidential Suite was standing wide open. All of the lights inside were turned on. There was no sign of the wheel chair, no sign of Amelia Corning.

"Now what?" Della Street asked.

Mason, standing in the doorway, said, "I would presume, Della, that, knowing she had an appointment with us, she left the door open so we could come in and be seated."

They entered the room. Mason gestured toward the half-open door to the bedroom. "Better see if she's in there, Della," he said.

Della Street flashed him a quick apprehensive glance, started to say something, then checked herself, moved toward the half-open door, knocked on it and called out, "Hello, Miss Corning. We're here."

There was no answer.

Della Street pushed the door all the way open, walked into the bedroom.

"Anybody home?" she called.

She heard quick steps and Mason was standing behind her.

The room gave evidences of feminine occupancy; an open closet door, dresses on hangers, creams on the dressing table.

Mason, beating a hasty retreat, said, "Look around, Della. Just be sure there's no one here. Try the closets—even under the bed."

"Chief," Della Street exclaimed apprehensively, "you don't think that—?" She checked herself and hurried toward the closet.

Mason returned to the parlor and seated himself.

Some two minutes later, Della Street returned and shook her head.

"Look every place?" Mason asked.

"Everywhere."

"The bathroom?"

"Yes."

"All right," Mason said, indicating a door at the other side of the parlor. "There's another bedroom there. Try that."

Della Street hurriedly opened the door, this time without knocking, again made an exploration and returned. "No one," she said.

"No wheel chair?"

She shook her head.

"How many suitcases?" Mason asked.

"I didn't notice particularly. I think there are . . . wait a minute, let me think. That's right, two suitcases and a bag."

Mason said, "I guess we wait."

Della Street seated herself. "Couldn't we ask the elevator operators?" she asked.

"We could," Mason said, "but we won't. Not right at the moment."

"One would have thought she'd have left a note," Della Street said.

"Well," Mason said, "she left the door open and—" He broke off as they heard the sound of voices.

"Someone coming down the corridor now," Mason said.

A rather portly woman in the middle forties appeared in the doorway. Behind her was a dapper individual with dark hair, dark eyes and a short mustache. Behind them were two bellboys with bags.

Mason got to his feet.

"I beg your pardon," the woman said. "I thought this was Amelia Corning's suite."

"It is," Mason said. "We are waiting for her."

"She isn't here?"

"Not at the moment," Mason said. "We had an appointment and found the door open. We assumed it was an invitation to come in and be seated. Permit me to introduce myself. I'm Perry Mason, an attorney, and this is Miss Street, my secretary. And you are . . . ?"

"I'm Sophia Elliott," she said. "I'm Amelia's sister. And this is Alfredo Gomez, her business agent."

"Oh, yes," Mason said affably. "I understand she was expecting you. She told me over the phone you were arriving, but I didn't think you were coming until later."

"We found we could catch an earlier plane," Sophia Elliott said, and turned to the bellboy. "All right," she said, "just bring the suitcases in."

Alfredo Gomez, slim-waisted, quick and catlike in his motions, came forward to bow low in front of Della Street, holding her hand in his for a moment, then crossed over to shake hands with Perry Mason.

"With much pleasure," he said.

Della Street glanced quickly at Perry Mason.

"I presume you talked with Miss Corning over the phone from Miami?" Mason said.

"We sent her a wire," Sophia Elliott said.

"Is it Miss or Mrs. Elliott?" Mason asked.

"It's Mrs. Elliott!" she snapped. "And I'm a widow, if it's any of your business—which it isn't."

Mason said, "I am representing a client who has had some dealings with Miss Corning, and Miss Corning asked me to meet her here." Mason looked at his watch and said, "Nearly ten minutes ago."

"Well, if she told you to be here ten minutes ago and she isn't here, she isn't intending to meet you here," Sophia Elliott said. "She keeps her watch accurate to the second and when she makes an appointment she keeps it. Now, where are we going to put these things?"

The question was addressed not to Mason but to the bellboy.

"There are two bedrooms in the suite," one of the boys said.

Sophia Elliott strode across the parlor to the bedroom door on the north, pushed it open, looked inside, came back to the parlor and without a word strode across to the other door, pushed it open, looked around, came back and said, "All right, Alfredo, you take that bedroom. Have the boy put your bags in there. There are twin beds in this other bedroom. I'll move in with Amelia."

Alfredo Gomez bowed his acquiescence, indicated a suitcase and a bag. "Those are mine," he said to the bellboy in a somewhat stilted English that was pronounced quite distinctly and without accent.

The bellboys took the baggage into the bedrooms. Sophia Elliott supervised the placing of the baggage in the one bedroom but Alfredo Gomez stood waiting, silently watchful while the boy deposited his bags in the other room.

Sophia Elliott returned, said to Gomez, "Tip the boys."

Gomez reached in his pocket, pulled out a roll of bills.

"That's Brazilian money. It's no good here," Sophia Elliott said.

Gomez let his white teeth flash in a smile at the bellboys as he replaced the currency in his pocket, reached into another pocket, took out a billfold and solemnly extracted a dollar bill which he tendered to one of the bellboys.

"That's not enough," Sophia Elliott said.

Gomez took out two more bills.

"That's too much," the woman remarked. "Give each of them one dollar."

Gomez gravely complied.

The bellboys, with impassive faces, muttered their thanks and left the room.

"I gathered," Mason said to Sophia Elliott, "that your wire came as something of a surprise to Miss Corning."

She pivoted slowly to regard Mason with an appraisal which lacked cordiality.

"You say you're an attorney?"

"Yes."

"Representing my sister?"

"No, representing someone who has business dealings with your sister."

"Were you invited in here?"

"I was told to be here at seven thirty."

"That's not answering my question. Were you specifically invited in here? I mean, right here in this room?"

"We found the door standing wide open," Mason said. "I took that as a silent invitation."

"What time is it now?"

"Nearly seven forty-five."

"All right," Sophia Elliott said. "She isn't here, she didn't leave any note for you. I'll tell her you called. If she wants to see you again she'll send for you."

"I beg your pardon," Mason said. "No one sends for me. I am an attorney."

Alfredo Gomez came gliding up to stand at Sophia Elliott's side.

"She sent for you this time, didn't she?"

"She asked me to call and I agreed to be here."

"All right. If you're so touchy about it," Sophia Elliott said, "if she wants to see you again she'll ask for you to call and you can agree to be here. That's all now. I'm moving in."

She walked over to stand by the door, holding it open.

Mason bowed. "It was a very great pleasure to meet both of you," he said, and stood aside for Della Street to precede him into the corridor.

"Humph!" Sophia Elliott grunted.

"And," Mason said, "you might tell Miss Corning that if she wishes to see me, I will be in my office at nine thirty tomorrow and she can telephone for an appointment."

They stepped out into the corridor and Sophia Elliott pushed the door shut.

Della Street raised quizzical eyebrows.

The lawyer smiled, took Della Street's arm and started with her toward the elevator.

"What one would call a rather dominating personality," Mason said.

"That," Della Street observed, "is quite an understatement. One wonders how Amelia Corning reacts to all this."

"One really wonders," Mason said. "Quite apparently she didn't send for her sister and the dashing Alfredo. They came of their own accord and presumably at their own invitation, and quite probably to protect their own interests."

"Evidently didn't want Miss Money Bags out of their sight," Della Street said.

Mason rang for the elevator. "One would gather that Miss Corning's sister has all the answers. Notice that she didn't ask the bellboy to put the bags in the parlor until Amelia Corning showed up. She simply moved right in."

"And proceeded to take charge," Della Street said.

The elevator cage slid to a stop and the door opened.

"Where now?" she asked.

"Now," Mason said, "we are going to see our client, Susan Fisher."

Chapter Eight

Perry Mason rang the chimes in Susan Fisher's apartment and received no answer.

He frowned at Della Street, tried the door. The door was locked. Again he sounded the chimes.

"I can't understand it," Mason said. "I told her to stay in her apartment and be where she could be reached instantly on the telephone."

"What do you suppose has happened?" Della Street asked.

"Whatever it was," Mason said, "it was something of sufficient importance to cause her to break the promise she made me and . . . unless, of course, she was confronted with some emergency and called Paul Drake. Let's see if she left a message there."

They went back down to the ground floor, found a telephone booth and called Drake.

"Perry Mason," the lawyer said. "What have you heard from Susan Fisher—anything?"

"She telephoned at six o'clock," Drake said. "She told me that something had come up which was so exceedingly confidential she didn't dare breathe a word of it, but that she was going to have to be out for a while. She asked me to relay the message to you."

"Did you try to pump her to find out what it was?"

"Yes, but I couldn't get to first base. She was evidently in a breathless hurry. She said to tell you things were going to be all right and for you not to worry."

"Okay," Mason said. "I'll keep in touch with you. She'll let you know when she gets back."

The lawyer hung up the telephone, emerged from the booth and shook his head in response to Della Street's unspoken question. "She's gone out," he said. "She left rather a cryptic message for Paul Drake. He said she was in a breathless hurry. Under the circum-

90

stances, Della, I guess we go and eat. Everybody seems to be standing us up tonight."

"Those," Della Street announced, "are words that ring musical chimes in my brain. Those words tinkle upon my eardrums with the effect of music—we eat."

Mason said, "Well, we'll do it on the installment plan, Della. I notice there's a cocktail lounge a couple of blocks down the street. We'll go down there, have a cocktail, then get back here in about twenty minutes, check on our client once more and then if she isn't in we'll go get a nice dinner."

Della Street said, "May I offer an amendment?"

"What is it?"

"Long experience with you has taught me that the bird in the hand is far, far better than two in the bush. In place of having a cocktail now and eats later, let's forget the cocktail and put in the half-hour at the restaurant around the corner. I would much prefer digesting a meat loaf in my stomach than to get through until midnight on the promise of a filet mignon. Meat is more nourishing than words."

"Okay," Mason said, laughing, "but I want to be back here within thirty minutes at the outside. There's something about this case which worries me."

They went to a little restaurant around the corner where the service was prompt. As Della Street had jokingly surmised, there was meat loaf and gravy ready for immediate service.

Within thirty minutes they were back and Mason had parked his car in front of Sue Fisher's apartment house.

Mason was escorting Della Street to the door when a slender figure in a long raincoat with a hat pulled low, started to push open the door, then suddenly stopped with a gasp.

"Mr. Mason!" Susan Fisher exclaimed.

Mason looked at the garb—the man's hat, the sweater, the slacks, the raincoat, the flat shoes—and said, "Now, what are you doing masquerading as a man?"

"I—I don't know," Susan Fisher said. "Oh, am I glad to see *you!* Oh, I—I was hoping that I could get in touch with you."

Mason said, "You could have been in touch with me if you'd only followed my instructions and remained in your apartment."

"I know, I know, but I couldn't."

"Why not?"

"Because she telephoned me."

"Who?"

"Amelia Corning."

"What did she want?"

"She wanted to do something without anybody knowing about it."

Mason's eyes narrowed. "What happened?" he asked.

"I . . . is it all right to talk here?"

"Probably not," Mason said. "Let's go up to your apartment . . . look, child, you're shaking."

"I know I'm shaking. I'm so nervous I feel like I could wilt on the doorstep."

The lawyer escorted her to the elevator, then down the hallway. Della Street said, "Let me have your key, dear, and I'll unlock the door."

After they had entered the apartment Mason said, "All right, Susan, let's have it."

Susan seated herself, started twisting her gloves nervously as though wringing water from them.

"Go on," Mason said encouragingly. And then added, "We may not have much time, you know."

Susan said, "She telephoned and told me exactly what to do. She told me to take a pencil and write down her instructions in shorthand."

"What were they?"

"I have them in my notebook but they're etched in my mind. She told me to go to the office of the drive-yourself car company that is only four blocks away, to rent an automobile, then to go up Mulholland Drive to an intersection she described, then on one and three-tenths miles to a service station. At the service station I was to go on down the road for another two-tenths of a mile. There was a wide place there and I was to park the car. Then I was to walk back to the service station and ask for a one-gallon can of gasoline. She said I was to take the can of gasoline, pay for it, take it down and put it in the car—that anyone driving at night should be equipped for any emergency."

"And *why* was all this?" Mason asked.

"She said that she wanted to get me to drive her to Mojave and she didn't want anyone to know what she was doing. She said she absolutely had to interview a man in Mojave before the banks opened tomorrow."

"Did she say why?"

"No."

"Or what name?"

"No."

"And what about the clothes you're wearing?"

"She said I was to get a man's hat that had a good broad brim, that I was to wear slacks, a sweater and a raincoat, that I must wear flat shoes so I could do quite a bit of walking, if necessary.

"And she told me the nicest things, Mr. Mason. She told me that she had checked very carefully on me, that she appreciated my candor and my straightforward sincerity as well as my loyalty to the company. She told me that she was going to throw Endicott Campbell out and that I was going to be placed in an executive position. She said—"

"Never mind all that," Mason said. "Tell me exactly what happened. What else did she say about instructions, and what did you do?"

"I did exactly as she told me. I knew that there was a broom closet here where the janitor kept some old clothes and I knew he had this broad-brimmed hat there, so I borrowed it. I had a heavy opaque raincoat. I left so that I got to the designated place on Mulholland Drive a good twenty minutes before the appointed time. I parked the car, went to the gasoline station, got the one-gallon can of gasoline and went back to the place and waited and waited and waited and waited."

"The man gave you the one-gallon can of gasoline," Mason asked, "the man at the service station? He didn't offer to drive you down to where your car was standing?"

"No. Miss Corning told me that if he did that, I wasn't to encourage him. She said she didn't think he'd do it, however, because only one man would be on duty."

"He didn't offer to drive you?"

"He wanted to, all right, but he said he was there alone. If there had been two of them, he would have driven me down. He even contemplated closing up the station long enough to drive me down there, but I didn't encourage him and . . . I guess he was afraid someone would come along and find the station closed and report it."

"What about the rented car?" Mason asked.

"I waited and waited, and when she didn't show up I took the rented car back and paid the rental. She had told me to do that if she didn't meet me there by seven thirty. She said if she wasn't there by that time I was to leave at once and return to the apartment, turning in the rented car. I asked what I should do with the can of gas and she specifically told me not to return it to the gas station, but to throw it in the bushes by the side of the road."

"Where did you get the money to pay for the car?"

"This other woman gave me money for expenses when I was working there at the office yesterday morning. Miss Corning told me to use that money and that she'd replace it."

"What time did she tell you she'd be there?" Mason asked, "at this rendezvous on Mulholland Drive?"

"She didn't tell me. She told *me* to be there by at least fifteen minutes past seven and to wait until *exactly* seven fifty. She said that she would join me during that interval if she could."

"When did this call come in?"

"About . . . oh, I guess it was five forty-five."

Mason glanced at Della Street. "That couldn't have been too long after we talked with her."

"She told me that she had talked with you on the phone, Mr. Mason. I wanted to know if she knew where I could reach you, and she said no, you couldn't be reached, that you were out of the city but that you'd telephoned her."

"You're sure it was her voice on the telephone?" Mason asked.

"Oh, yes, I'm quite sure. She has certain little mannerisms of speaking and I have a good ear for voices on the telephone. I'm quite certain it was she."

"You turned the car in and walked here from the car-rental agency?"

She hesitated.

"Did you?"

"No. Mr. Mason, I know I shouldn't have, but I was so upset . . . I stopped at the cocktail lounge and had a drink. I needed it."

"They know you there?"

"Yes. The bartender is very nice. I stop in there once in a while."

"How long were you there?"

"Not long—ten or fifteen minutes."

"Then you came here?"

"Yes."

Mason frowned. "The thing simply doesn't make sense," he said. "You can't fit it together any way so it does make sense . . . did Miss Corning tell you anything about her sister or her business manager from South America?"

"Not a thing," Susan said.

"Look here, Susan," Mason said. "This woman is from South America. She hasn't been here for years. She couldn't have given you all that detailed information. She couldn't have known about the distances, whether or not the attendant at the service station was alone, or—"

"Oh, but she could," Susan interrupted. "She said she'd engaged a detective agency and that all of these things were bits of a puzzle that would all fit together. She said the persons who had been planning to loot the company were planning a meeting that we were going to walk in on. She said that by the time you returned to town we'd have all the evidence you needed . . . and it was Miss Corning, all right. I knew her voice. There couldn't be any mistake."

Mason said, "I'm afraid you've either been a credulous little fool, or that Miss Corning has exposed herself to danger and may have been injured—and in *that* event you're really in trouble."

"But, Mr. Mason, what *could* I do? Absolutely everything depends on having the confidence and the backing of Miss Corning. I *couldn't* do anything except what I did. . . . She said her detectives had just reported and that there was no time to spare. She said she'd have given ten thousand dollars if they'd reported a little earlier and before you had phoned her. She said she thought you were in Mojave."

Abruptly Mason started pacing the floor, his eyes level-lidded with concentration.

"What's the matter?" Susan Fisher asked. "Do you suppose . . . ?"

Della Street, knowing the lawyer's habits of thought, motioned Sue to silence with a finger on her lips.

Mason paced back and forth for nearly two minutes. Suddenly he whirled. "All right, Sue, can you draw me an accurate diagram of the place where you parked the car?"

"Of course. She gave me a description in mileage and I took it down in shorthand and—"

"Where's the shorthand?"

"Right here."

"Have you transcribed it?"

"No."

"Do you have a typewriter here?"

"Yes."

"Write out the description," Mason said, "just as fast as you can. Then sit right here in this apartment. Don't leave until I tell you to, no matter *what* happens."

Spurred by the urgency of his manner, Sue Fisher uncovered a typewriter, ratcheted in paper and typed out the driving directions.

Mason studied the paper for a moment, folded it, shoved it in his pocket, said to Della Street, "Come on, Della."

"I'm to wait here?" Sue Fisher asked.

"Right here," Mason instructed, "and if Miss Corning phones find out where she is, then call Paul Drake and tell him. In the meantime, I'm going to phone Paul Drake to put a bodyguard on duty here."

"Suppose she phones and tells me to go out to join her and—"

"Find out where she is, phone Drake's agency, and then do exactly as she says. If you notice a man following you, don't be afraid. That will be Drake's man."

Mason hurried Della Street to the elevator, paused to phone instructions to Paul Drake from the booth in the lobby, then hurried to his car.

"We're going out there?" Della Street asked.

Mason nodded.

"Why? What do you expect to find?"

Mason said, "We *may* be in time to prevent a murder."

"Chief, you think . . . you mean . . . ?"

"Exactly," Mason said.

Ordinarily an exponent of careful, safe driving, Mason on this occasion crowded his car into speed.

"You'll be picked up," Della Street warned as Mason shot through a changing traffic signal.

"So much the better," Mason told her. "We'll impress an officer into service and take him along."

But there were no officers. The lawyer drove up on Mulholland Drive and started checking distances.

"This is the service station," Della Street said.

Mason, tight-lipped, nodded grimly, slowed his speed and moved cautiously down the road.

"Wait a minute, wait a minute," Della Street said. "That's the place right there, where she had the car parked, Chief."

"I know it," Mason said. "I don't want to leave *our* car parked there."

He drove on another hundred yards before he found a place where he could park the car. He took a flashlight from the glove compartment. "Come on, Della," he said.

The lawyer's long legs set a pace which forced Della Street to keep at a half-trot in order to keep up with him. They came back to the cleared place in the road where there were marks of tires in the soft soil.

The questing beam of Mason's flashlight moved around through the brush.

"Precisely what are you looking for?" Della Street asked.

Abruptly the beam of the flashlight answered her question as it came to rest on a red one-gallon can which had been thrown over into the brush.

"The gasoline can," Della Street said. "It must be empty!"

Mason nodded.

"Do we pick it up and . . . ?"

"We touch nothing," Mason said. "This way, Della."

Automobiles which had been driven through the low brush out toward the steep slope had made a roadway which consisted of but little more than two parallel lines of broken low brush.

Mason led the way to a point where there was a cleared space right at the edge of the steep slope. Petting parties had parked here, then turned their cars and gone back to the highway so that there had been left a circular space virtually devoid of vegetation.

Mason switched out the flashlight and listened.

From Mulholland Drive there was the occasional whine of a car. Far, far below, the noises of the city, muted by distance, furnished a rumbling undertone. A sea of twinkling lights stretched as far as the eye could see until a dark segment marked the location of the ocean. Overhead, stars blazed in tranquil steadiness.

"What a beautiful, beautiful spot," Della Street said. "Wouldn't this make an ideal—" She broke off abruptly with a half-scream.

Mason's flashlight, which had been switched on once more and was exploring the edges of the clearing, came to rest on a sprawled shape lying on its back in the unmistakably grotesque posture of death.

Mason moved closer.

The odor of raw gasoline permeated the atsmosphere.

The lawyer's flashlight came to rest on the features.

"Chief," Della Street said, half-hysterically, "it's Lowry—Ken Lowry, the manager of the mine."

Mason nodded. The beam of the flashlight continued to move.

"And here are account books," Della Street said, "all soaked in gasoline."

Mason nodded, approached the body of Ken Lowry. The lawyer bent over him and felt for a pulse.

"All right, Della," he said, "let's go."

"Chief, what happened? What . . . ?"

"We were too late to prevent a murder," Mason said. "We may have been early enough to have prevented the destruction of evidence."

"You mean fire?"

Mason nodded. "Let's be careful, Della. There's probably a cold-blooded murderer watching everything we do."

He retraced his steps to Mulholland Drive, took Della Street's hand in his and ran down to where he had left his car. He jumped in the car, drove it to the service station.

"Got a phone?" he asked the attendant.

The man nodded, motioned to a telephone.

Mason hurried inside, dialed police headquarters. "Homicide," he said.

A moment later, when he had the connection completed, he inquired, "Lieutenant Tragg happen to be there?"

"He dropped in for a minute and is just leaving. I can perhaps catch him in the corridor if—"

"Get him!" Mason shouted. "Tell him it's Perry Mason. Tell him it's important."

Mason heard a voice shouting at the other end of the line, "Hey, grab Tragg! Don't let him leave the building."

Several seconds later, Mason could hear the sound of footsteps approaching the telephone and Tragg's voice saying, "Yes, hello . . . Tragg talking."

Mason said, "You aren't going to like this any more than I do, Lieutenant. I've found a body."

"I see," Tragg said dryly. "And you are quite correct."

"In what?"

"In that I don't like it any more than you do, probably not as much. Now, where are you and what's it all about?"

Mason said, "The body is soaked in gasoline and I believe the murderer intended to set fire not only to the body but to some documentary evidence that is nearby. I'm going back and try to prevent it. Get officers up on Mulholland Drive just as fast as you can. I'm going to try and stand guard. I'll put Della Street on the telephone. She'll tell you where I am and how to get here."

Mason handed the phone to Della Street.

"You talk with him, give him directions," he said. "I'm going back."

"No, no," she cried. "It's dangerous. You can't . . . you're unarmed. . . ."

"Once this evidence gets destroyed," Mason said, "our client goes to the gas chamber. I don't think the murderer will start the fire if he knows there's a witness."

"He'll kill the witness," Della Street said.

"You tell Tragg how to get here," Mason said. "That's the best you can do. Tell him to rush up a radio prowl car first and then get up here himself."

The lawyer gave Della Street no more time to argue but dashed past the startled attendant at the station, jumped into his car, drove back to the wide place in the road, turned his car so that the headlights were shining down the road which had been made by petting parties, shut off the motor and rolled down the windows. He sat there watching the roadway, which was outlined in the beam of the headlights, listening intently.

Mason had waited some ten minutes when he heard the distant sound of a wailing siren. The wailing rapidly grew to a scream. The rays of a blood-red spotlight tinged the brush with a sinister glow, then etched Mason's car into brilliance.

The siren died to a throaty gurgle. An officer leaving the car came hurrying over to Mason's car, his hand on his gun.

"All right," he said, "what is it?"

Mason said, "I'm Perry Mason, the attorney. I telephoned Homicide and asked Lieutenant Tragg to get out here as soon as he could and to send a radio car out here at the first opportunity. There's a body over there about a hundred yards from the road and it's soaked with gasoline. I think the murderer intended to set fire to the body but was interrupted by my arrival."

"Oh, you do, eh? And how did *you* happen to arrive so opportunely?"

"I was running down a clue," Mason said.

"A clue to what?"

"A clue to an entirely different matter, although it may have been connected with the murder."

"Who's the person who was murdered, do you know?"

"To the best of my belief," Mason said, "the body is that of Kenneth Lowry, who was employed as manager of a mine operated by the Mojave Monarch Mining Company."

The officer hesitated a moment, then said, "You wait right here. Don't move. Don't go away. Don't get out of the car."

The officer went back and conferred with the other officer, then took a powerful hand flashlight and started walking down the road, being careful to keep to one side in the brush so as not to obliterate any tracks.

Mason sat there waiting.

Another twelve minutes passed and a second siren screamed in the distance. A short time later, another police car pulled to a stop. Lt. Tragg alighted, and crossed over to Mason's car.

"What's the idea, Mason?"

"I was reporting a body, that's all."

"Murder?"

"I would gather as much."

"Weapon?"

"I didn't see any."

"Identity?"

"I believe it is Kenneth Lowry, the manager of the Mojave Monarch Mine."

"You've seen him?"

"Yes."

"When did you last see him?"

"Late this afternoon. I saw him then for the first and last time."

"Where?"

"In Mojave."

"Then he must have followed you over here."

"He may have preceded me," Mason said.

"All right, what's your interest in the Mojave Monarch?"

"I was checking some of the financial affairs."

"Who for?"

"A client."

"Who's the client?"

"At the moment," Mason said, "I am not at liberty to divulge the client. However, I am going to make one suggestion, Lieutenant."

"What's that?"

"Amelia Corning was staying at the Arthenium Hotel. She seems to have left the hotel rather mysteriously. She had an appointment with me at seven thirty and she wasn't there to keep it. I have every reason to believe that prompt action on the part of the police may prevent *her* murder."

Tragg asked, "Where's the body?"

"Right down this little road," Mason said. "I've kept my headlights on the road and one of the officers from the radio car has gone down there and presumably is staying near the body to see that nothing is touched."

Tragg walked over to the radio car, conferred with the officer who was in that car, gave him some orders in a low voice, then returned to Mason's car.

"Come on," Tragg said to the lawyer, "let's go. Leave your headlights on. If your battery runs down you can get another one at this service station down the road. Let's keep some light on the scene."

Tragg walked over to the car in which he had arrived, said a few words and a photographer with a strobe light, a technician with a fingerprint case, emerged from the car.

Tragg said to Mason, "Lead the way, Perry. Keep off to the side of the road. Don't obliterate any tracks."

Mason said, "I've walked down here once before. At that time, I didn't know there was a corpse down here, so I left my tracks in the roadway. But when I came back I kept to the brush."

"Okay," Tragg said, "your tracks are here. Let's try not to leave any more."

Mason, picking his way through the knee-high brush to the side of the road, led the way down toward the clearing.

The flashlight of the officer from the radio car winked a signal.

"Over this way," the officer called.

Tragg and the group skirted the clearing, came to where the officer was standing.

"Lieutenant Tragg," Tragg announced. "What do you have here, Officer?"

"Evidently a murder," the officer said. "The body is soaked in gasoline and some books there are soaked in gasoline. There's a stiletto-type letter opener, that's evidently the murder weapon. I felt perhaps someone might be around here waiting to toss a match and set fire to the whole business so I was keeping guard."

"Good work," Tragg said. He turned to Mason. "All right, Mason, we'll furnish you with an escort back to your car. Don't leave until I question you."

"I'm going down as far as the service station," Mason said. "You can reach me there."

"Why the service station?"

"Della Street's there."

"All right. Go that far, no farther. Stay there."

Tragg said to the officer, "Take him back to the car. See he gets in the car and drives down to the service station. Keep him out in the brush, to one side of the road so he doesn't leave any tracks."

One of the men bending over the body said, "Lieutenant, this man hasn't been dead any time at all."

"But he's dead?" Tragg asked.

"He's dead."

"Okay," Tragg said. "Set up your photographic outfit and start getting some pictures. All right, Mason, this is where you came in."

The officer, holding Mason's arm, led the way through the brush, keeping well to one side of the road. When the lawyer had returned to his car the officer said, "Now, you're driving down to the service station."

"That's right."

"I'll follow you that far," the officer said.

"Okay," Mason told him.

The lawyer started his car, swung out onto Mulholland Drive, drove back to the service station. The police car followed behind him.

After Mason had swung in at the service station, the police car made a U-turn and went back.

Della Street smiled at Mason, opened her purse and took out some ragged bits of cloth.

"What's that?" Mason asked.

"One beautiful pair of nylon stockings cut all to pieces by brush. Is that a legitimate expense?"

"That's a legitimate expense for you and deductible for me," Mason said.

"It'll look nice on the expense account," she said. "One pair of nylon hose for secretary."

Mason grinned. "It won't appear on the expense account in exactly those words, Della. Let's get Paul Drake."

The service-station attendant came crowding forward eagerly. "Say, what's this all about?" he asked.

"A murder down the road," Mason said.

"Gosh, how did it all happen?"

"No one knows exactly," Mason said. "There's a gasoline can down there. You didn't sell anybody a gallon can of gasoline recently, did you?"

"Say, I sure did," the man said, "about an hour and a half ago, and I've been wondering what the heck happened."

"To whom did you sell it?"

"A young woman who was wearing a man's hat with a long raincoat. She kept the hat pulled down over her eyes."

"Blonde?" Mason asked, glancing significantly at Della Street.

"I don't know."

"A blonde, blue eyes, about five feet two and a half, about twenty-seven years old?"

"I thought she was younger."

"How much younger?"

"Well, I don't know. She *may* have been twenty-seven."

"Blue eyes," Mason said positively.

The attendant frowned. "Well, I don't know," he said. "I'm not entirely certain as to that."

"Then you didn't get a very good look at her?"

"No, I didn't get a very good look at her. She came in and wanted a gallon of gas. I remember wondering why she was wearing a man's hat and . . . well, I wondered just what was going on down there.

A girl being out alone that way, running out of gasoline—I wanted to drive her back down to her car, but I was here all alone."

"Rather a brassy individual?" Mason asked. "The kind who would be wandering around at night dressed in men's clothes?"

"I'm not so certain she was dressed in men's clothes. She had this raincoat and the hat."

"It was a man's hat."

"It was a man's hat, all right."

"Rather wide brim?"

"Wide-brimmed and she kept the brim sort of pulled down."

"But you could see her eyes were blue?"

"Now wait a minute. I'm not so certain about her eyes."

"You can't swear they were blue?"

The attendant hesitated and said, "No, I can't swear they were blue."

"Then you can't swear what color they were?"

"I . . . no, I guess I couldn't."

"Okay," Mason said. "Della, you talk with him, will you, and make notes on what he says? Try and get a description of this young woman."

Mason lowered his right eye in a swift wink. "I'm going to use the phone," he said to the attendant.

The attendant seemed only too willing to talk with Della Street.

Mason went over to the telephone, called Paul Drake's office. When he had the detective on the line, he said, "What's new with Endicott Campbell, Paul?"

"I think you're locking the stable after the horse has been stolen," Drake said. "We haven't been able to pick up his trail. He isn't at home and we can't find him."

"Keep trying," Mason said. "When you do find him, don't let him out of your sight—that's important. Now, here's something else, Paul."

"What?"

"We've simply got to find Carleton Campbell—that's the seven-year-old boy who's in the custody of this English governess, Elizabeth Dow."

"Have a heart," Drake said. "We're doing all we can on that, Perry."

"Do even better than that," Mason said. "There's been a murder.

Ken Lowry, the manager of the Mojave Monarch, has been killed. I was talking with him this afternoon. He must have got to thinking things over after we left and decided perhaps he'd told me too much, or else he put two and two together from things I had told him.

"Now, he may have started for Los Angeles to see Endicott Campbell or he may have started for Los Angeles to see Amelia Corning at the Arthenium Hotel. My best guess is that he went to see Miss Corning. He could have found out she was in town in some way; she might have telephoned him for all we know.

"Miss Corning has disappeared. She had an appointment with me at seven thirty and didn't keep it. She's a stickler for keeping appointments right on the dot. I want you to find out everything you can and I want to find it out fast."

"Where are you sitting in this thing?" Drake asked.

"More or less in the middle," Mason said. "I seem to have been playing tag with a murderer somewhere and I'm not sure who the murderer is."

"But you have a suspicion?"

"I have a suspicion," Mason said. "I'm going to need proof.

"Now, Amelia Corning's sister and her South American business agent have moved in at the Arthenium Hotel. Apparently the sister, Sophia Elliott, wears the pants in the family, or tries to. I don't think that goes too well with Amelia Corning.

"Now, here's something else that bothers me, Paul. I don't think that Amelia Corning was too anxious to have her sister and Alfredo Gomez, the business agent, show up. I think they showed up on their own initiative and there may be some friction, some adverse interest somewhere. It's just a hunch I have.

"I've given the police a tip to try and locate Amelia Corning. I told them that she was in danger of being murdered. That will spur them along."

"Do you think she *is* in danger?"

"I don't know," Mason said. "I just don't like the way these other people showed up, and I have a hunch Amelia Corning didn't either. When I talked with her over the phone and she told me that she'd received a wire from them saying they were coming, she didn't seem too happy about it."

"If you have the police working on the thing," Drake said, "there's not much I can do. The police will run circles around me."

"That's right," Mason said. "But you just might happen to stumble on something. I'll tell you one thing, Paul, that you *can* do."

"What?"

"Be so ostentatious about looking for her and so apprehensive that you build up a background of apprehension on the part of all concerned."

"*All* concerned?"

"That's right," Mason said, "*all* concerned."

"This is going to turn into quite a job," Drake said.

"It has turned into quite a job," Mason told him. "Get busy on it."

The lawyer hung up the telephone, noting as he did so that Della Street, with her wide and unmistakably beautiful eyes, had hypnotized the service-station attendant so that he had hardly noticed Mason had had a telephone conversation, let alone trying to eavesdrop on it.

Mason telephoned for a taxicab to come out to the service station, then joined Della Street, after a moment was able to get her off to one side where he could talk without being overheard.

"Della," he said, "I'm under orders from the police not to leave here. No one thought to give you any such orders. I've telephoned for a taxicab. It will wait here. You take my car and beat it."

"Where do I go?"

Mason said, "Della, this is important. I don't want the police to get on Sue Fisher's trail any sooner than they have to. On the other hand, I don't dare to have her resort to flight because that would be taken as an indication of guilt. Now, just suppose that you were told by me to go out and try and locate Miss Corning? Where would you go?"

"I don't know."

"It is quite a question," Mason said, "but we must bear in mind that she had some very involved mining interests out in the vicinity of Mojave. We must bear in mind that the murder of Ken Lowry has some rather deep significance. Now, if you should stop by Sue Fisher's apartment and take her with you so that she could brief you on the various things you wanted to know about, and if you should start for Mojave—well, of course you're rather tired tonight. I shouldn't ask you to work day and night. You've been going at a high rate of speed all day. You two girls could stop somewhere along the road at a motel. Of course you'd have to be careful to use your own names.

And then you could go out and look around Mojave tomorrow. There's just a chance . . . just a chance, that you could find something."

"You want delay, is that it?" Della Street asked.

Mason said, "Tut-tut, Della. You mustn't jump to conclusions. I am merely asking you to get evidence. I think you could get out there in Mojave, skirmish around and do a pretty good job."

"Do you want me to report to you?"

"From time to time," Mason said. "There's no use reporting to me tonight. Do you have plenty of money?"

"Not too much."

Mason reached for his billfold, took out two one-hundred-dollar bills.

"All right," he said, "this should keep you going for a while."

"How will you get along without your car?"

"Oh, I'll get along," Mason said. "I'll rent a car. You just take this and don't be in a hurry, Della. Telephone me from time to time."

"And if the police should catch up with us?"

"If the police should catch up with you," Mason said, "you might tell Sue Fisher that an attorney generally doesn't want his client to make *any* statement unless he is present, and he likes to talk with his client and know the facts before she makes any statements to the police."

"I think I understand," Della said. "Wish me luck."

"On your way," Mason said.

Della Street went to Mason's car, jumped in with a swirl of skirt and a generous flash of leg.

The service-station attendant watched her as she drove away. "Isn't that girl a picture actress?" he asked.

Mason shook his head.

"She should be," the attendant said dreamily. "The most beautiful girl I've ever seen in my life. Gosh, what eyes! And what a figure!"

Mason's smile was comprehensive. "And what competence," he said.

"What does she do?" the attendant asked.

"She's a very, very competent secretary," Mason told him.

The attendant stood looking down the road for a moment, then with a sigh went back to the interior of the station.

Chapter Nine

The taxi meter had nine dollars and eighty cents on it when Tragg somewhat reluctantly gave Perry Mason permission to go on about his business.

"I'm not very happy about this thing, Mason," Tragg said.

"One shouldn't ever be happy about a murder," Mason said.

"That isn't what I meant," Tragg said. "I'm not happy about any of them."

"All right, that's fine," Mason said. "You're not happy about any of them and you're not happy about this. That figures."

"Let's say I'm not happy about your part in this one."

"*I* have no part in the murder," Mason said.

Tragg jerked his thumb. "On your way," he said. "Personally, I think you've worked this professional privilege thing to death. I'm going to tell you something, Perry Mason. Sooner or later the facts in this case are going to come out. We're going to know how it happened that you went up there looking around for a body."

"I tell you, I wasn't looking around for a body," Mason said.

"All right, we don't need to go over it again. On your way."

Mason climbed in the cab, nodded to the driver. "Back down to Hollywood," he said.

After they reached Hollywood, Mason gave the driver the address of Susan Fisher's apartment and said, "There's a car-rental agency within three or four blocks of that apartment. Do you know where it is?"

The cab driver thought for a minute, then nodded. "There's a branch of the 'We Rent M Car Company' over on the boulevard that's only about three and a half blocks from there."

"Let's try that place," Mason said.

The driver drew up in front of the place. Mason went in and said, "How about renting a car?"

"It depends on how long you want it," the man said. "We're just closing up and business has been rushing today. This is a branch of the main office and we've been floored. I have one car which has just come in. It hasn't been serviced. I'll have time to fill the tank and that's all. If you want to turn it in before nine o'clock tomorrow morning, you'll have to turn it in at one of the other offices. I'll give you their address on a card."

"Okay by me," Mason said. "I need a car."

"You got your driving license?"

Mason brought it out and exhibited it, used an air travel card to establish credit and went out to pay off the cab.

"I was just closing up," the man explained. "We've had quite a day and I was fifteen or twenty minutes overtime getting books posted."

"Did a lot of rental business?"

"Quite a lot."

"You don't have too many cars?"

"Not here, this is a branch. Actually, we try to keep one here all the time and then we telephone to one of the other offices to send out replacements. They can have a car here within ten minutes any time I phone, sometimes sooner."

"Just keep the one car here in the place?"

"That's right. Of course, it isn't always the same car."

"I see," Mason said. "I was just wondering how you ran the business."

"Actually," the man told him, "this is kind of a business-getting gadget that the company is using. Some of our competitors are located at a garage somewhere in the city and then have a place at the airport. If you want to get a car, you have to go one place or the other, or arrange to have it delivered. And that makes it a little difficult when you want to return the car. We're trying out something new. We have places spotted all over town. You can either pick up a car here or I can have one for you within ten minutes and then I give you a list of places where you can leave it. You can turn it in at any one of these places; they're scattered all over town."

"Good idea," Mason said.

"It's working out all right for me," the man told him. "Of course,

I have a service station here. Let me fill up that gas tank and you'll be ready to roll."

While the gas tank was being filled, Mason crossed over to the telephone booth and called Paul Drake.

"Paul," he said, "I've got a car I want examined very, very carefully by an expert. I want someone who knows his way around to look it over with a magnifying glass."

"For what?"

"Bloodstains, fingerprints, everything."

"Well," Drake said somewhat wearily, "there's a technician who works in the police laboratory who occasionally does some work for me. He'll probably be in bed at this time of the night. I'll have to get him up if you want him."

"He'll keep his mouth shut?"

"He'll keep his mouth shut."

"He'll get up for you?"

"Not for me—for about fifty bucks."

"And work a large part of the night?"

"And work a large part of the night."

"Okay," Mason said. "Call him and then be waiting down on the sidewalk for me. I'll pick you up and we'll drive out there."

"How soon?"

"Fifteen minutes."

"Okay, I'll try and get things lined up," Drake said. "I'll be on the sidewalk. Anybody going to get any sleep tonight?"

"Not that I know of," Mason said. "Found anything on Amelia Corning yet?"

"Yes, we've got a lead. A fellow from the porter's office was paid twenty-five dollars to take Miss Corning down in the freight elevator in her wheel chair. She said she wanted to get out without anyone knowing it, said she had a little checking up to do."

"What time, Paul?"

"Six thirty."

"That figures," Mason said.

"What does?"

"She had an appointment with me at seven thirty and she's very punctual. She *could* have figured on getting back by seven thirty."

"That's right. She did. She made arrangements with this chap who operates the freight elevator so that he would be standing by in the alley, near the freight entrance, at exactly seven twenty so he could pick her up and take her back up to her floor and she could get into her room."

"And she didn't show up?"

"That's right. The fellow was there for all of ten minutes. She didn't show up."

"And she left at six thirty?"

"Right about that time. It could have been a few minutes earlier. The man says it could have been six twenty-five."

"Has he told his story to the police?"

"The police haven't asked him yet. They don't seem at all concerned—as yet. Our men saw no sign of police interest. Miss Corning's sister seems to be holding down the fort and clamping a lid on any undue interest in Amelia's comings and goings."

"That's good," Mason said. "We're evidently one jump ahead of the police. See what you can do about checking with taxicabs who usually stand there at the Arthenium Hotel and—"

"That's already been done," Drake said. "All of the taxicabs that stand there come in and take their position in line. They pull in to the rear of the line and then the fellow in front answers the doorman's signal. If the doorman isn't there, they'll pick up a passenger at the hotel and of course if the passenger walks up to the head of the line and gets in a cab, the cabby has no alternative but to take him. Ordinarily, however, they work with the doorman. In that way the doorman gets a tip for calling the cab and he's nice to the cab drivers and everything works out okay."

"And how about a cab being called around to the alleyway?"

"It would have had to have been on a telephone call," Drake said. "I've checked all the cab companies and there wasn't any call to have a cab there at that time. Therefore, it must have been a private car."

"It could hardly have been a private car," Mason said.

"It must have been."

"All right," the lawyer told him. "I'll come down there. I want this car checked for fingerprints and I want it checked for any and all kinds of evidence: A regular police check."

"That's going to take time."

"We've got time."

"I was afraid of that," Drake said, and yawned into the telephone.

"Get your man up out of bed," Mason said. "I'll be there, and be sure you're wearing gloves when I pick you up."

The lawyer drove the rented car around to his office building, picked up Paul Drake, who was standing on the curb. Drake gave directions and they drove out to the residential section, turned into a driveway and into an open garage.

"Meet Myrton Abert," Drake said. "He's an expert connected with the police laboratory."

"I want a check on this car," Mason said, "and I don't want anybody to know about it."

"You don't want anybody not to know about it any more than I do," Abert said. "It isn't hot, is it?"

"Not in the sense you mean. It's a rented car. I just want to know who's been driving it before all of the fingerprints are erased."

"Now suppose the police want the same thing?" Abert asked.

"Then you give them the information," Mason said.

"If I do that, I'll have to use Scotch tape and lift the fingerprints."

"Go ahead and lift them, but be sure you don't leave any indication prints have been lifted from the car."

"I don't see what you're gaining by this," Abert said.

Mason said, "Sometimes the police don't share information with me. If I share information with them, I'll at least be abreast of the police."

Abert thought it over, grinned, said, "Okay, I've got a fellow coming to assist me. He ought to be here any minute now. I had to get him up out of bed."

Abert closed the garage door, turned on bright lights and went to work.

It was breaking daylight when Abert said, "All right, Mr. Mason, there aren't any bloodstains in the car. There are quite a few smudged fingerprints. There are twenty-three legible fingerprints on the doors, the back of the rearview mirror and the side mirror. I've lifted those with Scotch tape. *Now* what do we do?"

"How are you on comparing fingerprints?" Mason asked.

"Pretty good."

Mason said, "I want duplicates of those prints."

"Then I'll have to photograph the lifted prints."

"How long will that take?"

"Not too long to make the photographs, but to get them developed and printed is going to be something else."

"All right," Mason said. "You want to protect yourself. You take the photographs and give me the original lifts. You can develop the photographs at your leisure. They'll give you protection."

Abert thought it over for a while, then said, "That would be worth a little more money, Mr. Mason. It's a little more work than I'd figured on."

Mason handed him a twenty-dollar bill.

"Will that cover the added costs?"

"That will cover it."

"Let's go," Mason said.

Abert walked over to a locker, took out a fingerprint camera, put the lifts on a dark surface, fitted the fingerprint camera over the lifts and within a few minutes had all of the prints photographed.

"That's all there is to it?" Mason asked.

"That's all."

"Okay," the lawyer told him. "I'm on my way."

"Say, this is a rent car, isn't it?"

"That's right."

"You understand I've got to protect myself in this thing," Abert said. "So far, this is only a private deal. But I've got the license of the car and all that and—"

"Sure," Mason said. "I don't want you to do anything that's going to get you in bad. You have a right to do outside work on your own time."

"Thanks. I just wanted to be sure we had it straight," Abert said.

"We've got it straight," Mason told him.

Abert looked at his watch and yawned. "Just about two hours' shut-eye before I have to go to work," he said.

"You're fortunate," Drake told him.

"In what?"

"In getting two hours' shut-eye," Drake said.

Mason grinned, opened the door of the car, slid in behind the steering wheel. "Come on, Paul," he said, "we're going places."

"Where?" Drake asked, as they backed out of the garage.

"Bed," Mason told him.

"Those," Drake said, "are welcome words."

"We stop by your office," Mason told him, "and see if they have anything more on any of the characters involved."

"Why not phone?"

"All right," Mason told him, "we'll phone."

They stopped at a telephone booth, Drake put through a call, came back and shook his head. "Nothing doing," he said, "they haven't found Endicott Campbell yet, there's no trace of the seven-year-old son or the governess, the police are turning Mojave upside down trying to get some dope on Ken Lowry, and, so far, the police haven't taken any interest in Amelia Corning. We're ahead of them on that information."

"Okay," Mason said. "It gives us about two hours and a half. We don't have to get up quite as early as your expert."

Chapter Ten

Perry Mason was up at seven forty five. He shaved, showered, dressed and, without breakfast, stopped at a supermarket, bought two dozen large, luscious eating apples, drove the rented car down to the front of a junior high school, parked it near the curb, let the air out of the left front tire until the tire was flat, and stood helplessly by the car until a group of students came along chatting and laughing, completely immersed in their own world and their own problems.

"Hey," Mason asked, "you boys want to make twenty bucks?"

The group paused and look at him suspiciously.

"Here are the car keys," Mason said. "I've got an appointment and I don't want to get all mussed up changing a tire. Fact of the matter is, I don't even know how to go about it. I don't know where the tools are. Here are the car keys and here's twenty bucks."

"What do you know?" one of the boys said.

"Manna from heaven," another remarked.

"I'm going to go over here to the snack bar and get a cup of coffee," Mason said. "I'd like to have you do the best you can with it."

Mason dropped a twenty-dollar bill on the seat of the automobile and walked across the street to the snack bar. "You boys help yourselves to some of those eating apples, if you want."

Looking back, he saw boys literally swarming all over the car.

By the time the lawyer had finished his coffee and walked back across the street, the tire was changed and one of the boys standing by the car said, "Gee, thanks a lot, Mister. We felt we shouldn't charge you that much. The boys felt they were sort of taking advantage of you."

"Not at all," Mason said. "I'm going to come out all right on this deal myself."

By that time, a crowd of some fifteen or twenty boys had gathered around the car, those who had not been in on the tire-changing deal looking enviously at those who had.

One of the boys said suddenly, "Say, I've seen you before. I've seen your picture someplace. Aren't you . . . my gosh, you're Perry Mason, the lawyer!"

"That's right," Mason grinned, and seating himself behind the steering wheel, left the door on the left-hand side of the car wide open while he visited with the boys for some four or five minutes. Then he closed the door and drove to his office.

He drove the car into the parking lot where he and Della Street kept regular stalls for their cars. Mason jumped out of the car and said to the parking-lot attendant, "I'm in the deuce of a hurry. Would you mind parking it in my stall when you get a chance? Thanks a lot."

Mason smiled his thanks and hurried to the elevators.

He stopped in at Paul Drake's office. "Paul in yet?" he asked the switchboard operator.

"Not yet," she said. "He left word that he was working until five o'clock in the morning and he was going to get a little shut-eye."

"Ask him to come in as soon as he shows up, will you?" Mason asked, and went on down to his own office. He went in through the reception room and told the receptionist, "Della Street probably won't be in today, Gertie. I'm going to be in my office for a while, but I may have to tell you to cancel all appointments."

Gertie, always the romanticist, said with awe, "Gee, Mr. Mason, it isn't another murder case, is it?"

"I'm afraid it is," Mason told her.

"And you're mixed up in it?"

Mason grinned. "Let's say we have a client who may become involved."

Mason walked back to his private office, seated himself and, picking up the phone, said, "Gertie, I want to get the Presidential Suite at the Arthenium Hotel. I'll talk with anyone who answers the phone. I'm afraid it's going to be rather a tough day today. We're going to have to get along without Della and—"

"Oh, no, we aren't. She's just coming in," Gertie said.

"What!" Mason exclaimed, jumping up out of his chair.

"She's just coming in."

Mason dropped the phone into its cradle, crossed the office with

rapid strides and jerked open the door to the private office just as
Della Street was about to open it from the other side.

For a long moment they stood there all but in each other's arms,
then Mason said, "Good gosh, Della, I'm glad to see you! Although
I suppose it's bad news."

"It's bad news," Della Street said.

"Come on in and tell me about it. Where have you been?"

"I," Della Street announced, "have been in the district attorney's
office since six o'clock this morning. We were routed out of bed by
deputy sheriffs from Kern County at a very early hour. Our friend,
Lieutenant Tragg of Homicide, showed up and started questioning
me in great detail."

"What did you tell him?" Mason asked.

"I told him the truth," Della Street said.

"All of it?"

"Well, there were some phases of the matter on which I didn't
elaborate, but I have never seen Lieutenant Tragg more insistent
and there was a deputy district attorney who was positively insulting."

"They didn't have any right to hold you," Mason said.

"That's what I told them. But they had an answer for all that.
They said I might be a material witness, that I might be aiding
and abetting a felony, that I might be trying to conceal evidence . . .
oh, they had lots of answers."

"Did they give you a rough time?"

"They were rather insistent," Della Street said, putting her hat in
the hat closet and dropping wearily into a chair. "I think the deputy
district attorney and one of the deputy sheriffs would have been
really rough in an insulting sort of way if it hadn't been for Lieutenant Tragg. He was probing and insistent, but very much a gentleman
of the old school."

"And what did Susan Fisher have to say?" Mason asked.

"As to that I wouldn't know," Della Street said. "They had her in
a separate room and they never let us have a word together from the
time they took us into custody. They brought her in, in one car,
brought me in, in another, and they interrogated us in separate
rooms."

"Well," Mason said, "I guess the fat's in the fire, the wind is about
to start blowing."

Gertie, in the outer office, gave a series of several short, sharp rings on the telephone and simultaneously the door from the outer office opened and Lt. Tragg stood smiling on the threshold.

"Good morning, Perry," he said, and turning to Della Street, bowed, said, "I've already seen you this morning, Della."

"You have for a fact," she said.

Tragg said, "You'll pardon me for walking right in without waiting to be announced, Perry, but as I've explained to you on several occasions, the taxpayers don't like to have us cooling our heels in the outer office and sometimes after a man knows we're waiting he takes steps which tend to defeat the purpose of our visit."

"And the purpose of your visit this morning?" Mason asked.

"Well now," Tragg said, "I was instructed to ask you to look at certain sections of the Penal Code."

"Indeed," Mason said.

"Sections having to do with concealing evidence, being an accessory after the fact, and things of that sort. But I'm not going to say anything about those sections."

"And why not?" Mason asked.

"Because," Tragg said, still smiling, "I'm satisfied you're familiar with them already, Counselor, and quite probably have taken steps to see that they don't apply."

"Then what *is* the purpose of your visit?" Mason asked.

"Right at the moment," Tragg said, "the purpose of my visit is to advise you that we're taking into custody a rented car which you picked up late last night from the We Rent M Car Company . . . and I'm instructed to ask you just why you deemed it necessary to rent that particular car."

"What particular car?" Mason asked.

"The one you rented."

Mason smiled. "The reason I rented a car was because Della Street had work to do and you had ordered me to remain at a service station. It therefore became necessary for me to call a taxi to take me back to town from the service station after you finished questioning me. Quite naturally one doesn't care to keep a taxi and pay taxi rates for ordinary driving. Even a fairly prosperous lawyer could run up too much of an expense account that way."

"I dare say," Lt. Tragg said. "I suppose you knew that the car you rented was the same one that your client, Susan Fisher, had rented earlier in the day and driven out to the place where the body of Ken Lowry was discovered?"

"No!" Mason exclaimed in surprise.

"You didn't know that?"

"How was I to know that?"

"You rented a car from the same agency."

"Certainly," Mason said. "I believe it was the nearest car-rental depot to the service station where you ordered me to remain."

"I see," Tragg said. "In other words, it was just one of those coincidences."

"You *might* call it that," Mason said.

"And again, I might not," Tragg said. "I'm quite certain the district attorney won't."

"All right," Mason said. "You want to pick up the car. I take it you'll give me a receipt, we'll check the mileage on the speedometer at the present time and I'll ring up the We Rent M Car Company and you can tell them that the police department is taking over and give them the mileage reading. I'd certainly hate to pay ten cents a mile for a lot of running around being done by the police department."

"Oh, certainly," Tragg said. "We're always glad to co-operate with you, Perry."

"Thank you."

"Now then," Tragg went on, "if we process this car for latent fingerprints and find that all of the fingerprints have been wiped from the car, it will be a very suspicious circumstance, Counselor. I think you can realize just how significant it will be and how suspicious."

"I wouldn't say that was a suspicious circumstance," Mason said, "but I am quite certain that by the time the prosecution gets done with it it will be made to appear highly significant."

"And it might leave you in a very embarrassing position," Tragg pointed out.

"It might," Mason agreed.

"You don't seem to think it will?"

"I'm hoping it won't, because I'm hoping that you won't find that the car has been wiped free of fingerprints."

"Well," Tragg said, "we've located it down in the parking lot and we have a couple of fingerprint experts going over it. If you don't mind coming down to the parking lot and checking the speedometer we'll give you a receipt for the car and then take over."

Mason signed. "Well, I suppose I'll have to. How long have you been working on the car?"

"Ever since you drove it in," Tragg said, grinning. "You know, Mason, I'm willing to make you a bet."

"What?"

"That the men report there isn't a single fingerprint on that car except perhaps one or two of yours by the door . . . and do you know what's going to happen if that is the case? I'm going to take you down to Headquarters for questioning, to find out whether you know anything about the fingerprints having been obliterated. I just thought I'd let you know so you could ask your highly competent secretary here to take care of canceling appointments in the event you don't return to the office."

Mason sighed and reached for his hat. "I always deplore these highhanded methods on the part of the police," he said.

"I know, I know," Tragg told him, "but the district attorney takes a very dim view of lawyers who go around obliterating evidence."

"Evidence of what?" Mason asked.

"Evidence of murder."

"What sort of evidence?"

"Well, for instance," Tragg said, "I wouldn't be too surprised if at one time Ken Lowry hadn't been in that car and that his fingerprints might have been found in the car if they hadn't been tampered with. For your information, Counselor, these fingerprint men are rather expert and if a car has been wiped free of fingerprints they can determine that fact—and, of course, since the car is in your possession, and since you would be the one who would have a strong motive to protect your client, the answer is more or less obvious."

"I would say rather less than more," Mason said. "Let's go down and take a look at the car, by all means. Perhaps you'd better come along as a witness, Della, so you can check the mileage."

"The more the merrier," Tragg said. "Let's go."

Tragg led the way out of the office and escorted Mason and Della Street down the elevator, out through the side entrance of the building and into the parking lot.

Two men were working feverishly over the automobile Mason had parked. Another man with a fingerprint camera was busily engaged in taking photographs.

"Well?" Tragg asked, as they approached the car. "You found that it had been wiped clean?"

One of the men turned to Tragg. His face contained an expression of complete exasperation. "In all of my experience, Lieutenant," he said, "I've never found a car with more fingerprints on it than this. The thing is fairly plastered. They're just all over the car—front, back, windshield, windows, steering wheel, rearview mirror—the thing is plastered with prints."

For a moment the smile faded from Lt. Tragg's face. Then he drew a deep breath and bowed to Perry Mason. "One has no respect for an adversary who is unworthy," he said. "It's going to give me a great deal of pleasure to return to the prosecutor and tell him that there was no reason to bring you in for questioning."

"You expected to find fingerprints on the car?" Mason asked.

"Well," Tragg said, "I didn't think that they'd find the car had been wiped free of *all* fingerprints. I was instructed to tell you that I was certain such would be the case, but somehow I had an idea it wouldn't be quite that easy. However, I hardly expected to find the car fairly crawling with fingerprints. Would you mind explaining how that happened?"

Mason shrugged his shoulders. "I guess quite a few people must have touched the car," he said. "Perhaps the police were looking it over before I brought it in."

"Don't be silly," Tragg said.

One of the fingerprint men who had been standing nearby said to Tragg, "It looks as though one of the national political parties had been holding a convention in the damn car. It's nothing but prints."

Tragg bowed, raised his hat in a gesture which might have been one of farewell to Della Street or might have been a gesture of respect to Perry Mason. "Under the circumstances," he said, "there is no reason to interfere with your activities of the day, Counselor. Good morning."

"Good morning," Mason said, and taking Della Street's arm, walked over to check the mileage on the speedometer.

"Seventeen thousand, nine hundred and forty-eight and two-tenths. Is that right, Lieutenant?"

"That's right," Tragg said.

"Make a note, Della," Mason told her.

Della Street made a note.

"Good-by, Lieutenant."

"Au revoir," Lt. Tragg said. "I will doubtless see you later on."

"Oh, doubtless," Mason told him, and escorted Della Street back to the office building.

As Mason and Della Street entered the elevator and waited for it to get a load, Paul Drake came hurrying in, signaled the elevator starter to hold the cage, and sprinted to get in just as the door closed.

"Hi, Paul," Mason said.

The detective jerked to startled attention, whirled toward the back of the cage, saw Mason and Della Street, and said, "Gosh, am *I* glad to see *you.*"

"Something?" Mason asked.

"Lots of somethings," Drake said. "I'll walk down to your office with you and tell you the news in the corridor. . . ." He glanced significantly at the other passengers in the elevator who were watching and listening with the curiosity of people who lead humdrum lives and obtain a vicarious thrill from time to time by eavesdropping.

Mason nodded and as the cage began to empty at intervening floors, moved over to join Drake so that the three of them left the elevator together and started down the corridor.

"They've arrested your client," Drake said.

"I know that," Mason told him. "They even had Della Street in custody for a while."

"Okay," Drake said, "I'm going to tell you something, Perry. They've got some sort of an absolute ironclad bit of evidence that I can't find out about, but I'll tell you one thing. This is once you're defending a guilty client."

"You're sure?"

"*I'm* not," Drake said, "but my informant is. I got a straight tip from Headquarters to tell you to get out from under on this case."

"I can't get out from under, Paul. I'm in too deep. What about the rest of it?"

Drake said, "I have Endicott Campbell located. He came home about five o'clock this morning. No one knows where he had been. He drove up in his automobile, entered the driveway to the garage, entered the house, and has been there ever since."

"What else?"

"Police now have a bulletin on Amelia Corning. She wheeled her chair out of the freight elevator last night and that's the last anyone has seen of her."

"This man who operated the freight elevator—do the police know about him and his waiting in the alley?"

"Oh, sure," Drake said. "Just as soon as they started an official search they inquired of all of the elevator operators and this fellow who runs the freight elevator told them his story."

"And they have no trace of her?"

"Not a trace."

"That's strange," Mason said. "A partially blind woman in a wheel chair could hardly vanish into thin air."

"Well, she did," Drake said. "And remember this is the second time within forty-eight hours. The first person, who was impersonating Amelia Corning, vanished; now Amelia Corning has vanished."

"One person," Mason said, "was impersonating Amelia Corning. Therefore it was a very simple matter for *her* to vanish. All she needed to do was to get up out of the wheel chair, take off the dark blue spectacles and be on her way. But with the real Amelia Corning it's a horse of another color."

The lawyer unlocked the door of his private office, stood aside for Drake and Della Street to enter, said, "All right, Paul. Now we've got to go to work. We've got a bunch of fingerprints to check."

"We're going to have the deuce of a time," Drake said.

"How so?"

"Police have a lot of power," Drake pointed out. "They can go to the man who runs the We Rent M Car Company and tell him they want his fingerprints. They can go to Endicott Campbell and ask if he has any objections to giving them his fingerprints. Then they compare those fingerprints with the ones in the car.

"We're in a different position. We've got a flock of lifts of fingerprints and all we can do is to eliminate certain ones gradually and then guess at the other ones. We don't have the power the police have."

"What about the man who took the prints? Do you suppose he will turn in the photographs to the police?"

"He will if he knows the police are looking for them."

"When will he know that?"

"Perhaps not for a day or two," Drake said. "It depends on how the publicity hits the newspapers. There's really something weird about this case, Perry, and don't underestimate Endicott Campbell. There's one smooth, fast, clever operator."

Mason said, "I made a mistake there, Paul. I should have had you keep a couple of shadows on him and find out where he went and what he was doing. Of course we had no way of knowing Amelia Corning was going to disappear."

"Naturally," Drake said.

"All right," Mason told him, "you get busy and find out everything you can. Get every possible scrap of information. In the meantime, take these lifts of fingerprints and try to match them up. By this time the police have booked Susan Fisher, so they'll have her fingerprints. The coroner will have taken the fingerprints of Ken Lowry. Whether we can find fingerprints of Amelia Corning is another question. I think they may have taken them in connection with her passport visa or some other governmental red tape in connection with immigration. They're probably on file somewhere."

"Suppose either Amelia Corning or Ken Lowry had been in that rented car," Drake said. "Suppose fingerprints are identified."

Mason thought for a moment, then slowly shook his head. "If either of them were in that car," he said, "we're licked."

Drake said, "Somehow I have a peculiar feeling in the pit of my stomach over this one, Perry. I think they're laying for you."

"Well," Mason said, "you won't have any difficulty getting the fingerprints of Ken Lowry. He's at the morgue. Get somebody working on that right away."

"I already have," Drake said. "Let me have the lifts and I'll go down to my office. I instructed my office to get fingerprints as soon as the coroner had made them."

"The coroner would let them go?" Mason asked.

"Sure," Drake said. "They handle that stuff as a matter of course. They fingerprint every corpse that comes in for autopsy."

"How was the murder committed, do you know?"

"A jab into the heart; a single stab wound, evidently a stiletto letter opener."

"Where was the point of entrance, front or back?"

"Side," Drake said. "It evidently caught Ken Lowry completely by surprise. He was with someone he trusted."

"All right," Mason said. "You start working on those fingerprints."

"I can check on Lowry's fingerprints within a few minutes," Drake said. "Let me call my office. I'll have the prints sent down here."

Drake called his office, said, "I'm in Mason's office. Did you get the fingerprints of Ken Lowry from the coroner? . . . Good. . . . Send them down, will you?"

Within thirty seconds Drake's switchboard operator was at the door with the set of fingerprints and Drake sat down at the desk. Mason got the lifts from his brief case and handed them to Drake.

Drake sat there with a magnifying glass, examining first one lift and then the other against the ten fingerprints which had been received from the coroner's office.

Suddenly Drake looked up, an expression of dismay on his face. "Hold everything, Perry," he said.

"What is it?" Mason asked.

"Let me make sure," Drake said.

He held one of the lifts a few inches above the print which had been received from the coroner's office, then slowly folded the magnifying glass, put it down on the desk, looked up at Perry and said, "This time you've done it. Ken Lowry's fingerprint was one of those lifted from the automobile.

"If you notify Lieutenant Tragg that you have that print you've given your client a one-way ticket to the gas chamber and if you don't notify him, you've put yourself in the position of concealing vital evidence in a murder case."

Mason thought the matter over for a minute, then said, "We'll do neither, Paul. Ring up your man who lifted the fingerprints. Tell him the car is figuring in a murder case and he should develop his photographs of the prints and take them to the police immediately."

"Without letting anyone know that you suggested he do so?"

"That's right."

"That makes you vulnerable on both flanks," Drake said. "The police have the information and you don't have the credit of turning over the evidence to the police as a potential defense."

Mason nodded. "We'll cross that bridge when we come to it, Paul. If the police start working on me they won't have so much time to work on Susan Fisher. I'll be a distraction."

"Don't kid yourself," Drake said lugubriously, "they'll take time to work on everyone, including me."

Chapter Eleven

As Judge Burton Elmer entered the courtroom from chambers and stood for a moment while the bailiff proclaimed that court was in session, interested spectators noticed that Hamilton Burger, the district attorney, had seated himself at the right of his deputy, Harrison Flanders. Word had spread around through the county offices like wildfire that this was one case where Perry Mason's client would be proven guilty so thoroughly that there could be no possibility the lawyer could win his case. Her ultimate conviction was considered a mathematical certainty, and there was not the slightest question that she would be bound over to the Superior Court after the hearing in Judge Elmer's court.

Moreover, it was rumored that immediately following Judge Elmer's order binding the defendant over to the Superior Court for trial, Perry Mason would be charged with having concealed material evidence and proceedings would be instituted against him.

One of the prominent columnists had gone so far as to predict in the morning paper that the case itself would be over in Judge Elmer's court within two hours, and that before night the lawyer would find himself in almost as much trouble as his client.

Hamilton Burger's demeanor indicated the solemnity of one who is officiating at a trial which can only result in the death sentence.

"People versus Susan Fisher," Judge Elmer said.

"Ready for the People," Harrison Flanders said.

"Ready for the defendant," Mason announced.

Flanders proceeded with the deft skill of a veteran trial attorney to lay the foundation of the case. He introduced evidence of the crime; the discovery of the body of Ken Lowry within a very short time after he had met his death; the introduction of maps and diagrams showing the exact location of the discovery; the identification

126

of the body by a member of the family; the background of his employment by the Mojave Monarch Gold Mining and Exploration Company; the fact that this company was a subsidiary of the Corning Mining, Smelting and Investment Company.

When Flanders had finished with the last of the preliminary witnesses he made a bold stroke.

"Call Endicott Campbell to the stand," he said.

Endicott Campbell came forward, was sworn, gave his name, residence, and his occupation as the General Manager of the Corning Mining, Smelting and Investment Company.

"Did you know Kenneth Lowry, the decedent?" Flanders asked.

"I had met him briefly shortly before his death."

"Were you familiar with the company, which to save time, we shall call the Mojave Monarch Mining Company?"

"In a general way."

"What do you mean by that answer?"

"The company of which I am manager sent remittances to the Mojave Monarch Mining Company for the purpose of underwriting operations."

"Do you know how much money had been sent this subsidiary during the last year?"

"Yes, sir."

"How much?"

"Two hundred and seven thousand, five hundred and thirty-six dollars and eighty-five cents."

"That is reflected on the books of the Corning Mining, Smelting and Investment Company?"

"It is."

"Was there some unusual development in connection with this Corning Mining, Smelting and Investment Company, which to save time I will refer to as the Corning Company?"

"There was."

"What?"

"Amelia Corning, the owner of some ninety per cent of the stock in the company, who has lived in South America for some years, was coming to this city for a personal inspection of the affairs of the company and the subsidiary companies."

"You're acquainted with the defendant?"

"Yes."

"She was in your employ?"

"That's right."

"For how long?"

"For a period of something over eighteen months."

"What was her capacity?"

"She was employed as my assistant. She was more than a secretary. She co-operated with me in running the affairs of the company."

"Calling your attention to Saturday, the third of this month, did you have a conversation with the defendant?"

"I most certainly did."

"Where did that conversation take place?"

"Over the telephone."

"Are you familiar with the voice of the defendant so that you can be sure it was the defendant who was talking?"

"Yes, sir."

"What was the nature of the conversation? What did she say?"

"She told me that Miss Corning, who was not due until Monday, the fifth, had actually arrived unexpectedly on the third; that she had been trying to get hold of me and—"

"Now wait a minute. You say that '*she*' had been trying to get hold of you. Do you mean Miss Corning or the defendant?"

"The defendant said that she, the defendant, had been trying to get hold of me but had been unable to reach me."

"What else did she state?"

"She stated that my son, Carleton, aged seven, had been at the office with his governess, Elizabeth Dow, and had shown her a shoe box which he had claimed belonged to me; that she had inspected the contents of this shoe box and found that it was apparently filled with one-hundred-dollar bills, representing a large sum of money; that she had placed this shoe box in the safe without counting the money."

"What else?"

"She further went on to tell me that Miss Corning had had her come to the airport and then she had taken Miss Corning to the hotel, following which Miss Corning had gone to the office and had spent some considerable time there going over the records and had actually removed some of the records from the office."

"All this was on Saturday, the third?"

"Yes, sir."

"Now, did you subsequently ascertain whether or not this was true?"

"I ascertained that at least in part it was not true."

"What did you ascertain was not true?"

"My son did not give her any box or any other receptacle containing any money, and Miss Corning was not at the office. A woman who *claimed* to be Miss Corning did register at the hotel and the defendant did conspire with this woman to turn over to her—"

"Just a moment," Mason interrupted, "I object to the word 'conspire' as being a conclusion of the witness and ask that it may be stricken."

"It will go out," Judge Elmer said. "Just relate the conversation and what happened as you know it."

"Well," Campbell said, "I, of course, made arrangements to get in touch with the defendant immediately and to get in touch with this Miss Corning. The person who was posing as Miss Corning promptly disappeared, the defendant showed up with Mr. Mason as her attorney and there was, I may say, a complete lack of co-operation as far as giving me any further information about the shoe box or container—whatever it was—that held a large sum of money."

"Now then, shortly prior to this time, had you been in touch with Ken Lowry, the decedent?"

"I had, and I also got in touch with him again immediately *after* this incident."

"What did you do?"

"I drove to Mojave."

"And interviewed Mr. Lowry?"

"Yes."

"This, then, was the second time you had met him personally?"

"Yes. The first time was around noon on Saturday, the third. The second time was nearly one o'clock in the morning on the fourth. That second conference lasted for about an hour."

"Was there some reason for not having met him prior to the third?"

"I had been instructed to concentrate on the real-estate end of the Corning Company's activities and not to bother myself with the Mojave Mine. I had been particularly instructed to leave this company entirely in the hands of Mr. Lowry."

"Who gave you those instructions?"

"Miss Corning."

"How?"

"In a conference over long-distance telephone."

"Now, you sent some two hundred and seven thousand dollars from the Corning Company to the Mojave Monarch during the past year. Were there any returns from that company?"

"Not directly to the Corning Mining, Smelting and Investment Company, but rather to a subsidiary company. I was advised by Miss Corning that the subsidiary company would make an accounting at the proper time."

"Now, when you saw Mr. Lowry, did you have any conversation with him about his activities?"

"I did."

"And what did he tell you with reference to money which had been forwarded by him or what he had done with the money which had been sent him by the Corning Mining Company?"

"Objected to," Mason said. "Incompetent, irrelevant and immaterial; not the best evidence; calling for hearsay and for a conversation not within the hearing of the defendant."

"If the Court please," Flanders said, "this is part of the *res gestae*. This discloses the reason that Lowry was murdered. This was an official conversation between an employee of the company and the manager."

"I don't care how official it was," Mason said. "It wasn't binding on this defendant. Moreover, it is now quite apparent that Lowry wasn't in the employ of the Corning Company in any way. He was receiving money from the Corning Company and quite apparently from the testimony he was doing something with it other than sending it to the Corning Company."

"That's exactly the point I want to prove," Flanders said.

"Prove it by competent evidence then," Mason snapped.

"I think the point is well taken," Judge Elmer said. "I suppose it's a matter of bookkeeping record, isn't it?"

"As a matter of fact, it is not," Flanders said. "It is a peculiar situation and it is because of this situation that Lowry was murdered. We can show by several persons what Lowry did with the money that was received."

"You can show what he *claimed* he did with it," Mason said, "but what he claimed isn't binding on this defendant."

"I think I will sustain the objection," Judge Elmer said.

"Very well," Flanders said, his manner ostentatiously indicating disappointment, but it was quite evident from Burger's manner that he had anticipated the ruling.

"Did you have a subsequent conversation that day with Mr. Lowry, a conversation which took place after you left Mojave?"

"I did."

"What time was that conversation?"

"Around five o'clock in the afternoon."

"Was that conversation a personal conversation or a telephone conversation?"

"It was over the telephone."

"What did Mr. Lowry say?"

"He told me that Mr. Mason and his secretary—"

"Now just a minute," Mason said, "I wish to interpose an objection to that conversation as hearsay, as being incompetent, irrelevant and immaterial and no proper foundation laid. There is no indication that the defendant was present or that this conversation, in whole or in part, was ever relayed to the defendant."

"I am referring to a conversation which took place between the decedent and this witness," Flanders said, "relating to statements which were made by Mr. Mason as attorney for this defendant."

Judge Elmer shook his head. "Unless you can show that this conversation was communicated to the defendant, or that she was present, or heard the conversation, the objection will be sustained."

"Very well," Flanders said. "Now, did you have any conversation with the defendant personally about this shoe box filled with money?"

"I most certainly did."

"Who was present at that conversation?"

"The defendant, Perry Mason acting as her attorney, and Miss Della Street, Perry Mason's secretary."

"And what was said?"

"I told her that there was no shoe box filled with money in the safe at the office as she had advised me was the case."

"And what did she have to say with reference to that?"

"Nothing, except to insist that my son had given her a shoe box."

"Your son is how old?"

"Seven years old."

"His name?"

"Carleton."

"And when did the defendant tell you the shoe box had been given to her?"

"She said that morning at the office Carleton, accompanied by his governess, Elizabeth Dow, had delivered the shoe box to her; that she had inspected it and found that it was filled with hundred-dollar bills."

"Cross-examine," Flanders said.

"You went to the office before this conversation you had with us to search for that shoe box?" Mason asked.

"I did."

"Why?"

"She had told me that my son had given it to her and stated that it was mine. I certainly wanted to investigate, both as a father and as an official of the company."

"And you were unable to find any such shoe box in the safe?"

"That is right."

"You opened the safe to look?"

"Yes."

"Was anyone with you?"

"No."

"Then it is only your word against hers."

Endicott Campbell gave himself the luxury of a triumphant grin. "So far, Mr. Mason," he said sarcastically, "It is my word against hers, and so far, at least, I am not accused of killing anyone to cover my defalcations."

Mason bowed. "So far," he said. "Thank you, that's all for the moment."

"Call your next witness," Judge Elmer said.

"Call Elizabeth Dow," Flanders said.

Elizabeth Dow, a woman who had an angular figure which she made no attempt to improve in any way, came striding flat-footed to the witness stand. She sat with immobile features as she awaited questions after giving her name, address and occupation.

"You are familiar with Carleton Campbell, the seven-year-old son of Endicott Campbell, the witness who has just testified?"

"Yes."

"Do you have some official connection with him?"

"I am his governess."

"Were you such on Saturday, the third of this month?"

"Yes."

"Did you take him to the office of the Corning Mining Company on the morning of the third?"

"I did."

"Who was there?"

"Susan Fisher, the defendant."

"Was there some conversation between Susan and Carleton?"

"Yes."

"You overheard this conversation?"

"Yes. Some of it."

"Was Carleton carrying anything when he came to the office?"

"Yes."

"What was it?"

"A shoe box."

"Do you know *of your own knowledge* what was in that shoe box?"

"I do."

"What was it?"

"A pair of black patent-leather dress shoes belonging to Endicott Campbell."

"How do you know what was in there?"

"There was some conversation before we left the house between Carleton and his father about a treasure box and Carleton asked his father if he could trade treasures. Carleton thought he had his father's permission to take this shoe box."

"There was only the one box?"

"That's right, only the one box that Carleton took from the house."

"Now, *how* do you know what was in it?"

"After we were in the automobile I took occasion to untie the box when Carleton was not looking. I wanted to find out just what was in it because naturally I felt in a way responsible."

"What was in it?"

"As I have stated, just a pair of black shoes."

"That's all. You may inquire," Harrison Flanders said with a little bow to Perry Mason.

"You were driving the car at the time?" Mason asked.

"I was not driving the car," she said. "I was in the car behind the steering wheel. I started the car, then I asked Carleton where his coat was. He had forgotten and left it in the house. I told him to go and get it. While he was in the house getting the coat I took occasion to untie the box."

"The box was tied up?"

"Yes."

"What was it tied with?"

"Some sort of a cord. I think it was a piece of fishline."

"And you looked inside the box?"

"I did."

"And then tied it up again?"

"Yes."

"And from there, where did you drive?"

"Directly to the office."

"Why did you go to the office?"

"I knew that the defendant intended to be there and I wanted to ask her to keep an eye on Carleton while I did some personal errands. I asked her to do that as a favor to me."

"And she consented?"

"Yes."

"Now, is there any chance that the shoe box could have been substituted at any time?"

"Not before we got to the office, no, sir. Carleton had that same shoe box with him and took it into the office. Any substitution would necessarily have been made by the defendant."

"That's all," Mason said.

"Call Frank Golden," Flanders said.

Golden was sworn and gave his occupation as proprietor of a branch of the We Rent M Car Company.

"Directing your attention to Sunday, the fourth of this month, did you see the defendant?"

"I did."

"Did you have any conversation with her?"

"Yes."

"And did you complete any transaction with her?"

"Yes."

"What was the transaction?"

"I rented her one of our units, a car designated on our books as Car Number 19."

"What time did you rent that car to her?"

"At six thirty o'clock."

"And did she return it to you?"

"Yes."

"At what time?"

"Our records show that it was eight fifteen."

"And that car was designated on your books as Car Number 19?"

"Yes."

"Is there a number painted on that car?"

"There is. It is rather inconspicuous but it has a painted figure of Number 19."

"Later on that evening did you have occasion to rent that car to anyone else?"

"Yes."

"Who?"

"To Mr. Perry Mason, the attorney for the defendant."

"What time was that?"

"Just before I was closing. Sometime around—oh, a few minutes before eleven. I put it on the books as ten thirty because that's the official time of closing."

"When you saw the defendant how was she dressed?"

"She was wearing a raincoat, a sweater, slacks and a man's hat; a broadbrimmed hat that was pulled down over her eyes. I thought at first she was a man but after she talked with me I saw, of course, she was a woman. And then of course I identified her from her driving license."

"She showed you her driving license?"

"Yes. That's necessary in order to rent a car."

"And your records show the name on that driving license?"

"Yes, sir. The name of Susan Fisher, the defendant in this case."

"When did you finally get the car back again?"

"It was on the afternoon of the fifth. It was returned by the police. I was notified that the police had taken possession of the car."

"That's all. You may inquire," Flanders said.

"No questions."

"Call Myrton Abert," Flanders said.

Myrton Abert gave his address and occupation and testified that after midnight, Sunday, at an hour around 12:30 to 1:00 o'clock Monday morning, he had been called by Perry Mason and Paul Drake to take fingerprints from a car; that he had noted the license number of the car and also the number 19 painted in an incon-

spicuous place. That he had lifted a series of fingerprints and delivered them to Perry Mason; that he had stipulated, however, that in
the event the car was concerned in any crime he would make the
information available to the police and that he had taken photographs of the fingerprints; that those photographs had been turned
over to the police; but that prior to the time they had been turned
over to the police, the police had appeared with a set of fingerprints
purporting to come from Ken Lowry, the decedent, and that one of
those fingerprints—that of the right middle finger—coincided with a
latent print which had been lifted from the automobile on the back of
the rearview mirror; that the witness was a fingerprint identification
expert and had made the identification; that there could be no question that this print had been made by the middle finger of the right
hand of the decedent.

"Cross-examine," Flanders snapped.

"No questions," Mason said.

"Call Lieutenant Tragg," Flanders said.

Lt. Tragg took the stand, testified to receiving a phone call from
Perry Mason reporting the finding of a body at the place shown in
the map indicating an area on Mulholland Drive; that he had first
ordered a radio car to proceed to the place at once and see that the
evidence was preserved. Then he himself with a deputy coroner, a
photographer and a technical expert had gone to the place; that
there they had found the body of Kenneth Lowry.

Tragg introduced various photographs and identified them.

"How long had the body been there? How long since death had
taken place?"

"A very short time," Lt. Tragg said. "I will leave it to the autopsy
surgeon to fix the exact time, but death had been quite recent."

"Now then, did you, in the course of your examination, look for
automobile tracks in the vicinity of the body?"

"I did."

"What did you find?"

"I found where a car had been driven over a rather faint roadway
leading into the place where the body was found. I carefully traced
the tracks of that car and made a moulage showing the tracks. I was
able to get good tracks of all four of the tires on the car. They had
rather distinctive treads."

"Were the tires all the same?"

"No, sir. The tires consisted of two different makes, two different types of tread. Those on the front were one make, those on the back were another make; and there was, moreover, a distinctive gouge on the tire on the right front which left a very distinct individual track."

"Did you subsequently find an automobile equipped with tires which matched the moulage?"

"Yes, sir."

"What automobile was it?"

"Automobile Number 19, owned by the We Rent M Car Company. I found this automobile parked in the parking lot of Mr. Mason's office building and Mr. Mason admitted to me that the car had been placed there by him, that he had rented it the night before from the car-rental company."

"You may inquire," Flanders said.

Mason's eyes narrowed. "Lieutenant, when did you find these tracks?"

"The night we discovered the body."

"How long after you discovered the body?"

"Only a few minutes, while you, I believe, were waiting at the service station."

"You said nothing to me about finding these tracks."

"No, sir."

"Why not?"

"I didn't realize I was under any duty to report to you as to what the police found, Mr. Mason."

"That's all," Mason said.

Flanders called Sophia Elliott to the stand. Sophia Elliott testified that she was the sister of Miss Corning, that she had traveled from South America, that she had gone to the suite of her sister at the Arthenium Hotel and that when she reached the suite she found the door open and found it occupied by Perry Mason and his secretary; that after some talk she had suggested that the door be closed and that Mr. Mason and his secretary leave and they would be notified in the event Miss Corning wanted to see them.

The man who operated the freight elevator testified to receiving twenty-five dollars for the purpose of smuggling Miss Corning out of the building.

Then came Harrison Flanders' surprise witness.

"I will call Carlotta Ames Jackson."

Mrs. Jackson proved to be a rather snippy, needle-nosed, nervous individual who quite evidently enjoyed the attention she had attracted.

"Where were you on the night of Sunday, the fourth of this month?" Flanders inquired.

"I was in the alley, back of the freight entrance of the Arthenium Hotel."

"How did you happen to be there?"

"I work in the hotel. I am a chambermaid. I come out of the back entrance and walk down the alley every night when I get off work."

"You were walking down there this night?"

"Yes."

"Did you notice anything unusual?"

"Yes."

"Describe it, please."

"I saw a woman in a wheel chair there in the alley. There is no sidewalk in the alley and this woman had her wheel chair right against the wall. It was an unusual place for a woman in a wheel chair and I started forward to speak to her."

"Did you speak to her?"

"No."

"Why?"

"Because a car turned into the alley, drove on past me and stopped right beside this woman. The driver of the car got out, helped the woman into the car, the wheel chair was folded up and put in the car and the car drove away."

"Did you see the driver of the car?"

"Yes."

"Was it a man or a woman?"

"It was a woman."

"Can you describe her?"

"She was wearing a raincoat, a sweater, slacks, and a man's hat which was pulled down over the eyes."

"Did you at any time see this woman's face?"

"Yes."

"How close were you to the woman at the time you saw her face?"

"I guess about twenty feet."

"Had you ever seen that woman before?"

"Not to my knowledge."

"Did you ever see her again?"

"Yes."

"When did you see her again?"

"At the police station."

"Who showed her to you?"

"There was a line-up of five women. I picked this woman out of the line-up."

"And who was this woman, if you know?"

"The defendant, the woman sitting there, Susan Fisher."

Susan Fisher gasped with horrified dismay.

"Did you have an opportunity to observe the make of the automobile?"

"Indeed I did."

"Have you seen that automobile since?"

"Yes. I subsequently identified it at the We Rent M Car Company. It had the number 19 painted on it to designate it."

"You may inquire," Flanders said with exaggerated courtesy, to Perry Mason.

Mason arose to face the witness. "Did you get the license number of this automobile at the time you first saw it?"

"I thought I did."

"You *thought* you did?"

"Yes, I'm quite sure I did."

"Did you write it down on anything?"

"No."

"You trusted to memory?"

"Yes, and I forgot it. By the time I was told that what I had seen might be of great importance in a murder case, I found I couldn't recall the license number."

"Did you see the number 19 on this car at the time it drove in the alley?"

"No."

"It was dark at the time?"

"It was dark."

"Were you standing near the car?"

"Within about twenty feet."

"You kept on walking?"

"No, I stood still."

"Why?"

"So I could see better."

"Couldn't you see better if you had been nearer?"

"Perhaps."

"Then why didn't you keep on walking?"

"I . . . Well, I just wanted to see what was going on, that's all."

"You are inclined to be curious as to things that go on around you, Mrs. Jackson?"

"I am *not!*"

"Then this was a new departure for you?"

"I don't know what you mean by that."

"Ordinarily you are not interested in things that go on around you?"

"Ordinarily I *am* interested in what I see."

"And try to remember those things?"

"Sometimes."

"You say that you identified the defendant in a line-up."

"Yes."

"Had you ever seen her before the line-up?"

"That time in the alley."

"Never before that?"

"Well, I had a glimpse of her when she was being escorted into the show-up room."

"Had you seen her picture prior to that time?"

"Yes. Police had shown me her picture and asked if that was the young woman I saw."

"And you told them it was?"

"I told them I . . . Well, I told them I thought it was."

"Did you first tell them that you couldn't be sure?"

"Well, of course. A body can't take a look at a picture and—"

"I'm asking you," Mason said, "if you first told them you couldn't be sure."

"Yes."

"Did you first tell them you didn't think that was the girl?"

"Well, I may have."

"But after you saw her in the line-up after the police had first let you get what you call a glimpse of her, you were positive?"

"Yes."

"Did you see the number 19 painted on the car at the time you saw it in the alley?"

"No, that was later."

"And how did you identify the car?"

"By its general appearance."

"That car was one of a popular make of automobile?"

"Yes."

"There are thousands and thousands of those cars of that same make and model, identical in appearance in every way, on the streets of Los Angeles?"

"Well, I don't know about thousands and thousands, but . . . well, anyway, I'm satisfied now it was the same car."

"*You're* satisfied," Mason said.

"Yes."

"How many conversations have you had with the police?"

"Oh, several."

"And with the district attorney's office?"

"Several."

"As many as ten with the police?"

"I guess so, first and last."

"As many as ten with the district attorney's?"

"No, only about five with the district attorney's."

"Now let's see," Mason said. "As I understand it, you weren't quite so positive at the time the police first interrogated you but with the passing of time you became more positive. Is that right?"

"Yes."

"You weren't positive the first time you were interrogated?"

"Well . . . No, I don't suppose I was. I told them I wasn't entirely sure. I had to keep thinking of it and a little more would come back to me each time I'd think of it."

"So with each conversation you had with the officers you became more positive?"

"Yes."

"That was the object of their conversations with you?"

"I don't know what the object was."

"But they had about ten conversations with you."

"Yes."

"And with *each* conversation you became more positive."

"Yes."

"So you weren't quite as positive at the time of the ninth as you were at the time of the tenth, or as you are now."

Hamilton Burger arose. "Your Honor," he said, "that is browbeating the witness. That's pettifogging. That's not legitimate cross-examination. That's not what she said at all."

"That is exactly what she said," Mason retorted. "She said she was more positive with each conversation and she had at least ten conversations. Therefore it follows that she wasn't as positive at the time of the ninth conversation as she was at the time of the tenth."

"I think I will overrule the objection," Judge Elmer said, smiling.

Hamilton Burger slowly seated himself.

"Now that the district attorney's objection has warned you of the trap, can you answer the question?" Mason asked. *"Were* you less positive at the time of the ninth conversation than you are now?"

"Well, that isn't the way I meant it."

"Never mind what you meant," Mason said, "I'm asking you a question. Answer it yes or no."

"No. I was positive at the time of the ninth conversation."

"Then why did you have the tenth?"

"I don't know."

"And why did you say you were more positive at the time of each succeeding conversation?"

"Well, I wasn't referring particularly to the time between the ninth and the tenth."

"All right, we'll go back to the eighth time," Mason said. "Were you more positive at the time of the tenth conversation than you were at the time of the eighth conversation?"

"Yes," the witness snapped angrily.

"And more positive at the time of the seventh than you were at the time of the sixth?"

"Yes."

"And more positive at the time of the fifth than you were at the time of the fourth?"

"Yes."

"Thank you," Mason said. "That's all."

Judge Elmer looked at the clock. "It is a few minutes after the hour of the noon adjournment," he said. "Does the prosecution anticipate there will be much more evidence?"

"No, Your Honor," Hamilton Burger said.

"Court will adjourn until two o'clock this afternoon," Judge Elmer said. "I have a brief matter which I am taking up at one thirty but I expect it will be concluded by two o'clock so that we can continue with this case. Court is adjourned and the defendant is remanded to custody."

Chapter Twelve

Perry Mason, Della Street and Paul Drake gathered in the private dining room of the little French restaurant near the Hall of Justice where they so frequently had lunch during Mason's court cases.

Mason looked around and said, "Well, we've had some very great near defeats here but usually during the lunch hour we've managed to get our heads together and squeeze out of the trap some way."

"This is one you're not going to squeeze out of," Drake said lugubriously. "Your client is guilty, Perry, and what's more, she probably lured Amelia Corning out someplace and disposed of her. I'm betting that within another twenty-four hours Amelia Corning's body is discovered somewhere, and when that body is discovered you'll find your client is charged with another murder."

"She may be charged with a murder," Mason said, "but that doesn't mean she's guilty."

"Perry, how can you say that? The evidence points so unerringly and so damningly that there isn't a ghost of a chance she's innocent."

Mason said, "That's because you're looking at the evidence from the standpoint of the prosecution. Now let's start doing a little detective work. . . . What have you been able to find about Ken Lowry's telephone calls?"

"No outgoing calls," Drake said, "and we haven't been able to trace any incoming calls."

"He had an incoming call," Mason said. "We know that he had one incoming call. That was from Endicott Campbell. Campbell has testified to that. Now then, Campbell either said something which started Lowry rushing to Los Angeles, or else there was another call right after Campbell's call. When Della Street and I left him, he had no intention of coming to Los Angeles. He must have received another call immediately after we were there and that call started him for Los Angeles. Now, we stopped to telephone you and to have a cup of coffee. We just made it to the Arthenium Hotel by seven twenty-five. Lowry simply couldn't have reached the city much before that time. Even if he'd received an immediate telephone summons, he couldn't have got here much before seven forty-five."

"All right," Drake said. "Your client met him as soon as he arrived, took him out and murdered him and was back with the car by eight fifteen."

"It doesn't leave her enough time," Mason said. "She would have had to have Lowry meet her at the scene of the murder."

"Well, is anything wrong with that?" Drake asked. "Lowry returned to his cabin at the mine. There was a call waiting for him. The voice of Susan Fisher, a voice he had come to know, instructed him that he'd pulled a boner talking with you and told him to drive to Hollywood at once, then go to this designated spot. Your client had written out the directions in shorthand.

"You and Della went to Los Angeles, to the hotel, then out to Hollywood. Lowry could have taken a shortcut through Burbank and saved at least half an hour."

Mason said, "We're going to have to find out about that call. Let's see if we can trace it down."

"If we do," Drake said, "we'll find it was a call from your client and . . . well, then what are you going to do, Perry? Are you going to try to suppress the evidence or are you going to put it in the hands of the officers?"

"That," Mason told him, "brings up a difficult question of ethics. An attorney shouldn't suppress evidence. On the other hand he shouldn't go around digging up evidence against his client. However, the evidence *may* not be against my client. How about giving your office a ring and see if they've uncovered something?"

Drake called for a telephone which was plugged in, gave the number of his office to the operator, said, "Hello. Paul Drake talking. What have you found out? . . . Okay, let me have it."

Drake's eyes narrowed. He made notes, said, "Okay. I'm here at the usual restaurant, in the private dining room. Call me if anything turns up."

Drake hung up the telephone, said to Mason, "Well, we've got it but it's a peculiar lead."

"What is it?" Mason asked.

"Long distance from Los Angeles was calling Kenneth Lowry on Sunday afternoon, probably at about the time you were talking with him at Mojave. Lowry didn't answer his telephone so word was left for him to call Operator 67, Los Angeles. A Mexican woman who cleans up the house remembered marking down 67 on the pad by the telephone.

"Well, we got in touch with Operator 67 and managed to trace the call. It was a call that was placed from a telephone booth. It was a woman's voice and the woman said she would wait until he answered. Evidently this woman sat there by the phone booth for some twenty minutes before the call was completed. It was a paystation call, and the woman deposited toll charges. Now then, Perry, the location of that telephone booth is within two blocks of your client's apartment. She evidently didn't want to put the call through from her apartment so she walked two blocks and put it through from a telephone booth."

"What name was given?" Mason asked.

"She told the operator it was a Miss Smith calling."

"I wonder if the police have that," Mason said.

"No, I don't think so, Perry."

Mason's eyes narrowed. "Now we know why Lowry drove into town. He drove in to meet somebody. It was a matter of major importance because he must have left the minute he got that telephone call. He must have been right behind us on the road."

"And Susan Fisher picked up Amelia Corning there in the alley," Drake said, "and went off with her, then picked up Ken Lowry. We know what happened to Lowry. . . . Good heavens, Perry, this woman must be a fiend. In order to cover a defalcation of a large sum of money she's committed two murders and—"

"Now, wait a minute," Mason interrupted. "Let's not condemn her of two murders before we know what the evidence is. She tells me that she absolutely did not have Ken Lowry in the car with her that night; that she had never met Ken Lowry; that she doesn't know what he looks like; and she tells me that she didn't pick up Amelia Corning there in the alley."

"Phooey!" Drake said. "There's too much evidence against her. My gosh, Perry, but you're an optimistic fighter. Almost anyone else I know of would have folded right there in court this morning with all this irrefutable evidence coming in. . . . Gosh, you could see Hamilton Burger just sitting there and beaming. This is one case that he has dead open-and-shut and he had to come to court personally so that he could have his picture in the papers when Mason loses a case."

"We won't be losing a case," Mason said. "This is just a preliminary hearing. The only purpose is to determine whether there is sufficient evidence that a crime has been committed and evidence that tends to connect the defendant with the commission of the crime."

"I know," Drake said, "you can explain it with all the legal technicalities you want, but remember in the popular mind it's a case, and one that you've lost."

"He hasn't lost it yet, Paul," Della Street said sharply, looking at her watch. "He's got an hour and thirty minutes before he's lost anything."

Mason said, "There are certain things about this case that puzzle me."

"Such as what?" Drake asked.

"Oh, the way this woman acted who showed up at the airport Saturday morning. . . . Of course, that was an unusual procedure, sitting there in a wheel chair with her baggage all around her. . . . I wish we could find out more about that woman."

"She was a ringer," Paul Drake said.

"But a clever ringer," Mason pointed out, "and she was very adept at the use of a wheel chair. She could send it whizzing around. . . ."

"How do you know?" Drake asked.

"Susan Fisher described it to me in detail," Mason said.

Drake's smile was skeptical. "I wouldn't build any hopes or any case on anything that was said by Sue Fisher," he said. "Personally, I think the girl is deranged somewhere. She's probably some kind of congenital psychopath."

"What additional evidence does the prosecution have?" Della Street asked.

"Only the murder weapon," Mason said. "They'll put that in, they'll tie that up with Susan Fisher, and then they'll rest."

"Are you going to put on any evidence?"

"I don't think so," Mason said. "There's no use putting on Susan Fisher and letting her deny all this stuff."

"You try to put her on the stand and Hamilton Burger will rip her to pieces on cross-examination," Drake warned. "That's why Burger is sitting so smugly in court. If you don't put your client on he's going to have the credit of winning a case in which you've fallen flat on your face. If you do put her on he's going to be the one who rips her to shreds."

"Ordinarily," Mason said, "there's nothing to be gained by putting a defendant on the stand in a preliminary hearing but . . . Hang it, I wish I knew something more about that ringer who took the part of Amelia Corning."

"She went to the Union Station," Drake said, "and simply disappeared. She didn't go out in any taxicab. Therefore she must have gone out in a private car. Someone was there waiting for her, and she probably simply took off her dark blue glasses, got up out of the wheel chair, folded the wheel chair and walked around just like any other normal human being."

Abruptly Mason snapped his fingers.

"What?" Drake asked.

"There's one thing you didn't try," Mason said.

"What?"

"Chartered limousines."

"What do you mean?"

"For a short trip you take a taxicab," Mason said. "For a long trip you charter a limousine with a driver. Ring up your office, Paul. Get them to cover the different limousine services. See if they received a call on Saturday afternoon after five o'clock to make a trip to Mojave."

"To Mojave?"

Mason nodded.

"Why Mojave?" Drake asked.

Mason, suddenly excited, got up from his chair and began pacing the floor. "I've got an idea, Paul," he said. "It's a terrific idea."

"You mean that there never was any other woman? That your client, Sue Fisher, was the one who was masquerading as Amelia Corning and she removed the make-up and—"

"Get your office on the phone," Mason interrupted him impatiently. "Have them cover the limousine services."

Drake put through the telephone call, instructed his office to cover the situation, then hung up the telephone.

"Well," Della Street said, "I don't know about you folks but *I'm* going to eat."

Drake sighed. "I think I better take aboard some groceries while the moment is opportune. Sad experience teaches me that these cases take unexpected twists, subsequent developments always result in greasy, soggy hamburger sandwiches in place of well-cooked meals. This time I'm going to fool everyone."

They gave their orders to the waiter, settled down around the table and after the food was served ate in moody silence.

At twenty minutes past one the telephone rang for Paul Drake.

Drake listened, made notes, said, "Okay, I guess that's it."

He hung up the telephone, turned to Mason and said, "Okay, Perry, you're clairvoyant."

"Go on," Mason said, his manner showing suppressed excitement. "Let's have it."

"Saturday afternoon, five fifteen, the A to Z Limousine Service received a call to have a limousine at the garage entrance at the Union Depot. They were instructed to have the limousine full of gasoline and be ready to make a trip. The driver went there as per instructions and picked up a woman in a wheel chair—a woman who had dark blue glasses. She gave him keys to some lockers at the depot. He went there and picked up her bags and suitcases, put them in the car and then drove her to Mojave."

Mason looked at his watch, his eyes narrowed. "All right," he said, "let's get back to the courtroom. I'm going to have to do a little cross-examination and then we may know more than we do now."

"Oh, for the love of Mike," Drake said wearily, "quit butting your head against a brick wall, Perry. This is a case where there's only one thing for you to do. Get up the minute court opens and suggest to the judge that while you think your client has a good defense, in view of the evidence that has been received there certainly is enough evidence to warrant binding the defendant over, and ask the court to make the order. In that way you'll steal some of Hamilton Burger's thunder and keep him from standing up and making an argument that will be directly primarily to the newspapers.

"That's all Burger wants. Just an opportunity to stand up and speak his piece. He'll argue about this young woman with her mask of innocence. He'll talk about the satanic character that lurks underneath. He'll thunder denunciations. He'll intimate that there is still another body waiting to be discovered, and he'll have his picture in the paper.

"After all, Perry, this thing . . . this limousine business doesn't really *mean* anything. We all know that there was a ringer brought in to take the part of Amelia Corning on Saturday and what more natural than that she should have been brought in from Mojave. I will admit my face is a little red because I didn't think of that limousine business but the police didn't think of it either. This driver of the limousine had never been interrogated before."

Mason didn't waste time answering Drake. He called the waiter, signed the check and said, "Come on, let's get up to the courthouse. We've got work to do."

Chapter Thirteen

Back in the courtroom Mason, waiting for Judge Elmer to return to the bench, said suddenly, "Paul, I want to find out who Endicott Campbell's female friends are."

"He doesn't have any," Drake said.

"Don't tell me that," Mason told him. "Of course the guy has woman friends. His wife left him two years ago and—"

"He had one for a while," Drake said. "That was before Susan Fisher came to the office. This woman was his secretary. She was a married woman. He had quite a crush on her and apparently it was reciprocated. At least, her husband thought so. He made quite a stink about it, threatened to shoot Campbell, and got the woman out of the office."

"They're not seeing each other now?"

"No."

"He doesn't call on any women?"

"Not since we've been shadowing him, Perry."

"Then he's wise to the fact that he's being shadowed. No telephone calls? No women coming to the house?"

"Only one woman has called at the house," Drake said, "and that's a friend of Elizabeth Dow, the governess."

"The fact that she's a friend of the governess doesn't keep her from also being a friend of Endicott Campbell," Mason said.

"Not this one," Drake said. "Here, I'll give you the dope on it." He took a notebook from his pocket, opened it, said, "Cindy Hastings, 1536 Rentner Road. That's the address of the Tulane Apartments. She's in 348. A nurse. Built something like Elizabeth Dow, the governess, only a considerably older woman. Angular. English. Flatfooted. Long-legged. Flat-chested. Horse-faced . . ."

"That's enough," Mason said. "Cross her out, but it's a nice lead.

151

What other friends does the governess have? People about her own age?"

"Apparently none," Drake said. "At least we've been unable to uncover any. I have an idea they're probably wise to the fact that we have shadows on them. They haven't given us any inkling that they know but they must have some idea and they're certainly being circumspect. They—"

A policewoman brought Susan Fisher into the court. As she seated herself behind Mason's chair she leaned over toward the lawyer and said, "You think I've let you down, don't you, Mr. Mason?"

"Frankly," Mason said, "I don't know."

"Well, I can tell you one thing, Mr. Mason. That testimony is a mass of lies. I never knew Ken Lowry in his lifetime. I never had him in that automobile. I have told you the exact truth at all times. I—"

Judge Elmer entered from his chambers and the bailiff pounded his gavel to bring the court to order.

Hamilton Burger seated himself at the prosecution's table, permitted a swift glance of triumph at Mason, then lowered his eyes to some papers on the desk.

Harrison Flanders said, "If the court please, our next witness is Norma Owens."

Norma Owens identified herself as the manager of the office of the Corning Mining, Smelting and Investment Company.

Flanders said, "I show you a stiletto letter opener marked People's Exhibit G, and ask you if you can identify that."

"That particular letter opener is one that was on the desk of the defendant, Susan Fisher. She used it to open letters."

"How do you identify it?"

"By its general appearance, and a little nick at the edge of the handle. I remember when that nick was put in there. Miss Fisher was using it to pry the lid off a can of paint."

"No further questions of this witness," Flanders said. "You may cross-examine."

"No cross-examination."

"I will recall Lieutenant Tragg for another question," Flanders said. "You have already been sworn, Lieutenant Tragg. Just take the stand."

Mason, looking out the window, his eyes focused on distance, seemed hardly aware of what was going on.

"You have made a search of the apartment of the defendant in this case, Lieutenant?"

"I have."

"Among other things were you looking for a receipt for renting Car Number 19 from the We Rent M Car Company?"

"I was."

"Did you find it?"

"I did."

"Does it bear the signature of the defendant?"

"It does."

"Will you introduce it, please!"

Tragg produced the paper.

"I ask that it be introduced in evidence as People's Exhibit R," Flanders said. He turned to Mason. "Cross-examine."

Mason apparently didn't hear what Flanders had said. His eyes narrowed in thought, he was staring out through the window.

"You may inquire, Mr. Mason," Judge Elmer said.

Mason gave a little start, said, "Yes, Your Honor. Thank you."

He rose to his feet, approached Lieutenant Tragg, who turned to face him expectantly, then said abruptly, "No questions," and returned to his chair.

"That's all, Lieutenant," Flanders said. "That's our case, Your Honor."

Hamilton Burger got to his feet. "If the Court please," he said, "I wish only to comment on matters which have been received in evidence but the Court will notice that we have here a murder—a coldblooded, deliberate murder. In addition to that we have the disappearance of Amelia Corning. This is a very serious matter and there is no question but what the murder and the disappearance are related."

"Just a moment," Mason interrupted. "Are you preparing to argue the case now?"

"Certainly," Hamilton Burger said.

"I doubt if there's any need for argument," Judge Elmer announced.

"Isn't it proper," Mason asked, "to give the defense a chance to put on evidence?"

Burger looked at him in surprise. "There isn't any evidence you dare to put on, none that you *can* put on."

Mason said, "If the Court please, before being called to put on any evidence on my side of the case I would like to recall Endicott Campbell for further cross-examination."

"We object to it," Hamilton Burger said. "This is a favorite trick of Counsel, to wait until the testimony is all in so that he is familiar with the case of the prosecution and then recall some key prosecution witness for further cross-examination."

"I think I will permit it, however," Judge Elmer said. "While this is a preliminary hearing for the purpose of determining whether there is reasonable cause to connect the defendant with a crime, the fact remains that it is a hearing in a court of law. The defense cannot be expected to know all of the prosecution's case. It is the theory of the law that the defense be given every opportunity to explain the facts."

"If the Court please, these facts are susceptible of only one explanation," Hamilton Burger said, "and I feel that Mr. Mason's desire to further cross-examine Mr. Campbell is simply for the purpose of gaining time and laying a foundation for some possible conflict in the evidence when the case comes on for trial in the Superior Court. We have certainly established a *prima facie* case and are entitled to a ruling of the Court at this time. If Mr. Mason wants to call Endicott Campbell as his own witness he can do so."

Judge Elmer shook his head. "I'm going to permit Counsel to recall Mr. Campbell for cross-examination," he said. "Take the stand, Mr. Campbell. You have already been sworn."

Mason said, "I just want to ask you a couple of questions, Mr. Campbell. You learned over the telephone from the defendant that your son, Carleton, had given her a shoe box containing a large number of hundred-dollar bills. You learned this Saturday night. Is that right?"

"I learned nothing of the sort," Campbell said indignantly. "She *told* me that my son had done that. I didn't learn that he had, because he hadn't. She told me a lie. I proved it was a lie. I instituted an investigation and found that my son had done nothing of the kind, that he had a shoe box containing a pair of my dress shoes. I know that my son kept some of his own toys or treasures, as he called them, in a shoe box, and I remember that I laughingly told him that we might trade. But I at no time had any shoe box containing any sum of money concealed in my house, and he at no time had any shoe box containing any large sum of money which he gave to the defendant."

"However," Mason said, "you were afraid to have the boy interrogated on this point so you had him spirited away out of sight where the police couldn't interrogate him, didn't you?"

"I did nothing of the sort!" Campbell shouted. "I certainly didn't intend to let you hypnotize my son and brainwash a seven-year-old boy in order to—"

"Now just a moment, just a moment," Hamilton Burger said. "There is no need for Mr. Campbell to volunteer any information, although I can appreciate his righteous indignation. However, if the Court please, this cross-examination is ill-advised, improper, calling for matters which are incompetent, irrelevant and immaterial."

"I think it may go to the bias of the witness. I'd like to know just what happened there," Judge Elmer said. "There's no reason why the witness can't answer the question. He seems to be taking care of himself all right."

Hamilton Burger sat down.

Campbell said, "That's all I have to say. I certainly didn't intend to have some smart attorney trying to make my son a football in an embezzlement case. I admit that I told Elizabeth Dow, the governess, to take him where he would be undisturbed by persons who wanted to question him and to remain away until I advised her to return."

"But how were you going to let her know when it was all right for him to return if you didn't know where they were staying?"

"I told her to call me up from time to time."

"I have no further questions," Mason said.

"That concludes our case," Hamilton Burger announced.

"I would like to recall Elizabeth Dow for further cross-examination," Mason said.

"We object, Your Honor. Counsel is now apparently going on a fishing expedition."

"Apparently so," Judge Elmer ruled. "Perhaps, Mr. Mason, if you would state the line of cross-examination you wish to pursue, the Court could make a different ruling."

"I want to find out where Endicott Campbell's seven-year-old son was kept hidden from Saturday evening on," Mason said.

"I don't see why," Judge Elmer said.

"It may make quite a difference in the case," Mason said.

Judge Elmer shook his head. "I think not. The permission to re-call Elizabeth Dow is not granted. Now do you have any defense, Mr. Mason?"

"If the Court please," Mason said, "I am going to ask the Court to take a recess until four o'clock this afternoon. At that time I will either proceed to put on a defense or I will submit the case without a defense."

"Why do you ask for this delay, Mr. Mason? Surely you must be aware, as a veteran trial attorney, that the evidence is so over-whelming against your client that there is absolutely no possible showing that the defense could make which would justify the Court making an order releasing the defendant.

"This is not a hearing where it is necessary to prove the defendant guilty beyond all reasonable doubt. It is only a hearing for the pur-pose of determining whether a crime has been committed and if so, if there is reasonable ground to believe that the defendant committed the crime. Those conditions certainly have abundantly been met."

Hamilton Burger, not to be denied an opportunity to make a few remarks, was on his feet. "Furthermore, if the Court please," he said, "I feel that *two* murders have been committed rather than one. I feel that this defendant should be shown no consideration. We have here a very revolting situation of a young woman who has betrayed a posi-tion of trust and confidence to loot the company which employed her. Then she had the temerity to try to cover her defalcations by in-gratiating herself with the principal stockholder of the corporation which employed her. Failing in that, she resorted to murder in order to cover her tracks. We know of one murder she has committed and I think the Court will realize from the evidence that the probabilities are two murders have already been committed."

"The defendant is in custody," Mason said. "She isn't going to com-mit any murders while she's in jail. I feel that I am entitled to an hour and a half to work on a theory of the case which I have and which I will state to the Court may well result in clarifying certain issues which need to be clarified. I can give the Court my professional assurance that I have reason to believe that I can uncover evidence of the greatest importance in the next hour and a half."

"Under those circumstances," Judge Elmer said, "and being well acquainted with Counsel's reputation, the Court is inclined to take his assurance."

"I'm also well acquainted with Counsel's reputation," Burger shouted. "It's a reputation for trickery."

"For ingenuity," Judge Elmer corrected. "An ingenuity coupled with integrity. There are times when his ingenuity may be exasperating to the prosecutor's office, but as far as this Court can observe, the integrity of Counsel has never been questioned. The Court is going to grant the motion. The Court will recess until four o'clock. The defendant is remanded to custody."

Mason beckoned to Della Street and Paul Drake, barged rapidly over to where Lt. Tragg was sitting. "Lieutenant Tragg," he said, "may I see you for a moment on a matter of considerable urgency?"

Tragg hesitated a moment, then said, "Well, why not?"

"This way," Mason said.

The lawyer led the way to the elevator. The four of them hurried into the cage well ahead of the vanguard of spectators.

"Run it all the way down," Mason told the elevator operator, "right to the ground floor quick. It's a matter of emergency."

"Hey, wait a minute," Tragg said. "What's happening here?"

Mason said, "We're going to have to do something before anyone realizes what we're doing."

"Now wait a minute," Tragg protested. "I'm not on your side, Mason. I'm on the—"

"Do you or do you not want to enforce the law and protect the citizens of this community?" Mason asked.

Tragg grinned at him. "No need of making a speech. I'm for motherhood and against sin. I'll ride along with you, Perry, but I'm warning you I'll lower the boom on you."

"Lower away," Mason said.

The elevator stopped at the ground floor. Mason headed toward the door, stretching his long legs so that Paul Drake was hard put to keep up, while the short legged Lt. Tragg, and Della Street were almost trotting.

The lawyer led the way to where the cars were parked.

"You've got a police car here, Lieutenant?" Mason asked.

Tragg nodded.

"Let's use it," Mason said. "You do the driving. Use the red light and a siren."

"I can't do that except on a major emergency," Tragg said.

"This *is* a major emergency," Mason told him. "You're going to get evidence that will be determinative if you get there before it is destroyed."

"You mean evidence that will clear your client?" Tragg asked dubiously.

"Evidence that will conclusively point to the murderer, whoever that murderer may be," Mason said. "I'll give you my word on that, Tragg. I've never lied to you yet."

Tragg said, "Okay, come on. This is irregular but I'm doing it."

They climbed into Tragg's car. Tragg started the motor and after they reached the street, turned on the red light and siren. "Where to?" he asked.

"1536 Rentner Road," Mason said. "The Tulane Apartments. We want Apartment 348."

"What's there?" Tragg asked.

"Evidence," Mason said.

Tragg said, "Okay, I've stuck my neck out this far, I'm going to ride along with you, Perry. But this is going to have to be good."

Mason said, "It will be good."

Tragg's siren cleared the way across intersections. The police lieutenant, having reached a decision, went all the way and barreled through red lights and boulevard stops, avoiding the congested freeway in order to make time on the streets which were not so filled with traffic.

When the police car was within half a dozen blocks of the Tulane Apartments Mason said, "Better stop the siren, Tragg. We don't want to unduly alarm anyone."

Tragg kicked off the siren and glided the last block and a half up to the curb.

Mason had the door open almost before the car was stopped and dashed into the apartment house. They piled into the automatic elevator. Mason pushed the button for the third floor. The cage rattled slowly upward, Mason manifesting his impatience.

They hurried down the hallway to Apartment 348. Mason knocked on the door.

A few moments later the door opened to the limit of a safety chain. A woman's voice said, "Who is it?"

Mason said, "Police. This is Lieutenant Tragg of Homicide. We want to come in and question you."

"You can't come in," she said.

"This is police business," Mason said.

"Now wait a minute," Tragg protested. "I—"

"Do you have a warrant?" she asked.

"No," Tragg said, "and furthermore I—"

Mason, backing back across the corridor, suddenly hurled himself at the door.

The hasp holding the safety chain pulled out. The screws jerked out a section of the wood as the door banged open.

Mason shot past the startled woman, ran through a sitting room and slammed open a door to a bedroom.

A woman was sitting groggily on the edge of the bed, holding onto the brass post of the foot of the bed. As Mason, followed by Lt. Tragg, entered the room, she said drowsily, "Don't let them . . . Don't let them . . . Don't let them shoot any more drugs into me."

"Who's this?" Lt. Tragg asked.

Mason said, "This is Amelia Corning, and if you'll look sharp you can get the woman who was in this apartment before she makes it to the elevator. If you don't, you—"

Tragg took one look at the woman on the bed, then whirled.

He was too late. The woman who had been in the apartment had sprinted down the corridor. Seeing the elevator was not in place she had taken to the stairs. Tragg started after her.

Mason sat down on the bed beside the woman and said, "Are you able to talk, Miss Corning?"

"Could I have coffee?" she asked. "Been doped . . ."

Della Street said, "I'll get some coffee on. There should be some in the apartment. Come help me, Paul."

The woman on the bed weaved around, then groped over toward Mason for support, put her head on his shoulder and promptly dropped into a deep, drugged sleep.

Ten minutes later Lt. Tragg came back to the apartment.

He found Mason and Della Street supporting the woman, who was drinking coffee from a cup held by Paul Drake.

"Did she get away?" Mason asked.

Lt. Tragg's mouth was grim. "She did not!"

"She beat you to the street, didn't she?" Mason asked.

"She beat me to the street," Tragg said, "but she didn't beat modern police methods. I got in my car, got the dispatcher on the line and we sewed the district up. We had radio cars converging on it from every direction and I was able to describe her, the dress she was wearing, her age, height, weight, appearance. . . ."

"You got all that," Mason asked, "in the brief glimpse you had?"

"Sure, I got all that," Tragg said. "What the hell do you take me for? I'm a cop but I'm not a dumb cop. That's police training. Your woman was picked up within three minutes after she hit the street, and she's on her way to Headquarters now, where she'll be held for questioning. Now tell me what it's all about and what I question her about."

"That woman," Mason said, "will turn out to be Cindy Hastings, a nurse. She posed as Miss Corning, wearing dark glasses and sitting in a wheel chair. She telephoned Susan Fisher and told her to put on a raincoat, slacks, a sweater, and wear a man's hat pulled down low over her forehead, and go to a place on Mulholland Drive and get a gallon can of gasoline from the service station."

"And then Susan Fisher picked her up in the alley?" Tragg asked.

"Picked her up, nothing," Mason said. "Cindy Hastings simply sat in the wheel chair at the alley. Elizabeth Dow, dressed exactly as they had told Susan Fisher to dress, came and picked her up. As it happened, a witness saw the pickup—and you know how fallible eyewitness testimony is, particularly when it comes to the identification of a stranger. The witness saw some woman in a raincoat with a man's hat pulled down over her eyes and imagination and clever police suggestion did the rest.

"So then the two women went to meet Lowry. Within a short time after they picked him up they were ready to go ahead with their murder, having carefully planned the details so Susan Fisher could never convince anyone of her innocence.

"I must have missed the murder by only a few minutes."

"Then the real Miss Corning," Tragg said, "was the woman who . . ."

"The woman who came Saturday," Mason said. "We should have known it if we'd done any great amount of thinking. That woman was very adept in the use of a wheel chair. She did everything that the real Miss Corning would have done and none of the things that the spurious Miss Corning would have done.

"The two women kidnaped her when she tried to get out to Mojave to look at the mine. They let her get as far as Mojave and then they drugged her, brought her back to Los Angeles and kept her con-

cealed here. In the meantime, knowing that Ken Lowry was going to
state that he could identify the voice of the woman who had told him
to ship currency to the Corning Affiliated Enterprises, they decided
they needed Lowry out of the way. And how could they do it any
better than by framing the crime on Susan Fisher?"

The woman on the bed smiled drowsily. "Can't see well," she
said, "but . . ." She yawned prodigiously, nodded, then straightened
and said, "Have a good ear for voices . . . whoever you are, you're
smart."

Mason said, "Everything is going to be all right now, Miss Corning. I'm Perry Mason, an attorney who is going to help you."

Mason turned to Tragg and said, "They were planning to use the
substitute Miss Corning and make it appear that the real Miss Corning was an imposter. But then Miss Corning's sister and her business
agent wired they were coming from South America to be with her,
and that necessitated a hurried change in plans."

The woman on the bed struggled to wakefulness. "So Sophia came,
did she? . . . Pain the neck . . . so damned afraid I'm going to
meet some fortune hunter and get married." Again the woman
yawned.

"All right," Tragg said. "Now tell me about the money and I'll put
the rest of it together by myself."

"I can't be sure about the money," Mason said. "Probably Campbell had a pair of shoes in a shoe box somewhere. Also, Elizabeth
Dow was keeping *her* money in a shoe box. Campbell told his son
they could trade treasure boxes and the boy inadvertently got the
box with all the money in it Elizabeth Dow had stolen from the mining
deal. She didn't know it until after she heard Campbell talking over
the telephone with Susan Fisher. Then she knew Carleton had got *her*
cache of money instead of his daddy's treasure—a pair of shoes."

"And what happened to the box of money?" Tragg asked.

Amelia Corning yawned, tried to say something, yawned again,
smiled, said, "I've got it . . . put it where they'll never find it . . .
not until I get ready . . . more coffee?"

"That's all there is to it," Mason said. "Elizabeth Dow, because of
what she had learned while working as a governess, saw a wonderful
opportunity to feather her nest. She rang up Ken Lowry, told him
she was Miss Corning calling from South America, told him to do a
lot of things that any sane businessman wouldn't have done. But

Lowry, being a square-shooting miner, accustomed to the outdoors and to dealing with people whose words were as good as their bond, and knowing that there may well have been a tax angle involved, followed instructions to the letter.

"Elizabeth Dow rented a post-office box under the name of Corning Affiliated Enterprises.

"Lowry was loyal enough so that he . . ." Mason looked at his wrist watch and said, "We're going to have to give this woman some more coffee, Lieutenant. We're going to have to get her to a doctor and we're going to have to use your official car in order to get all of us to court before four o'clock."

Chapter Fourteen

Mason came hurrying into court exactly at four o'clock, just as Judge Elmer, impatient at the delay, was taking the bench.

"Do you wish to put on a defense, Mr. Mason?" Judge Elmer asked.

"I do," Mason said. "I would like to recall Frank Golden, proprietor of the We Rent M Car Company, for a few questions on cross-examination."

"We object!" Hamilton Burger shouted. "Here we go all over again. We—"

"The objection is sustained," Judge Elmer interrupted. "If you have a case, Mr. Mason, put it on."

"Very well," Mason said. "I will call Frank Golden as my witness and then, if I may have the indulgence of the Court to make sure that my next witness has recovered from her drugged condition, I will call Amelia Corning as my second defense witness."

"Call who?" Hamilton Burger shouted.

"Amelia Corning," Mason said, smiling. "Frank Golden, will you take the stand, please? You've already been sworn."

Golden took the witness stand.

"You rented this car to the defendant Sunday night," Mason said. "She brought it back. After that, I rented the car. Did the car go out *after* the defendant brought it back and *before* I took it out?"

"I am afraid it did," Golden said. "I was busy when the defendant brought it back. I made a note of the mileage, but I didn't clear the records. I left the car parked out in front. Later on, when I went to look for it, it was gone. I assumed that my assistant had taken it and parked it. Later on, I found out he hadn't done so."

"How long was the car gone?"

"About an hour. It was returned shortly before you rented it and the speedometer showed it had been operated some thirty miles."

"You said nothing about this?" Mason inquired.

"I wasn't asked," the witness blurted. "And since it might get me fired, I decided I wouldn't say anything unless I *was* asked."

"Thank you," Mason said.

Della Street entered the courtroom and handed him a note.

"If the Court please," Mason said, "a physician states that Miss Corning is unable to take the stand. I think, however, I will call Lieutenant Tragg as my next witness."

Tragg, who had been whispering at the counsel table with Hamilton Burger, started for the stand. But the district attorney got to his feet, took a deep breath and said, "Your Honor, it will not be necessary. I wish to move at this time for a dismissal of the case against Susan Fisher and ask that she be released from custody."

Hamilton Burger sat down.

There was a moment of stunned silence, then reporters, who had in some way been alerted to the fact that there would be spectacular developments, started pellmell from the courtroom in such an exodus that Judge Elmer had to wait for a few seconds before smiling down at Susan Fisher and saying, "The motion is granted. The case against the defendant is dismissed . . . and thank you, Mr. Prosecutor, for your attitude in the matter."

Mason got up, picked up his brief case, turned and was suddenly smothered by a veritable avalanche of feminine enthusiasm as Susan Fisher, with her arms around his neck, crying and laughing at the same time, said, "Oh, you wonderful, wonderful man!"

Della Street, standing slightly to one side, smiled and said, "So say we all of us."

"But I can never, never, never pay you," Susan Fisher said tearfully. "Heaven knows how much you've spent and—"

"Don't worrry about that," Della Street said. "He had a hunch. He said all along that Miss Corning would pay the bill."

Lieutenant Tragg, moving up along side of Mason, said, "All right, Perry. Your client is in the clear. There is no longer any reason to hold out anything. How did you know?"

Mason said, "When a veteran trial lawyer examines a witness, Lieutenant, he gets a pretty good idea of whether that witness is telling the truth. When I asked Endicott Campbell about that money in the shoe box and about his son, I suddenly found that his answers were ringing true.

"I had cast him as the villain in the piece because he was a typical smug, overbearing little man trying to be big by bullying the office help. But it happened that on that shoe box full of money he was telling the truth.

"If he was telling the truth, then Elizabeth Dow had to be lying. And once *that* possibility confronted me, I suddenly saw the facts of the case in an entirely new perspective. It's like one of those optical illusions where you see a flight of black stairs going up and then suddenly something snaps in your brain and you find you're looking at a flight of white stairs going down.

"*One* of the two spinsters had to be an imposter. We had assumed the first one was, but she was adept in the use of the wheel chair, and the minute I learned she had checked out of the hotel in order to make a secret trip to Mojave I realized that *she* had to be the genuine one. A spurious Miss Corning would never have wanted to go to Mojave.

"Once it dawned on me that Elizabeth Dow was lying and that the real Amelia Corning had disappeared, I suddenly remembered that my investigations had disclosed Elizabeth Dow had a friend who was a nurse and whose physical appearance dovetailed exactly with that of Amelia Corning.

"As soon as I reasoned that far, I knew all the answers.

"Lowry had told me he thought he could recognize the voice of the woman who had given him his instructions over the telephone and had acknowledged receipt of the money from time to time. That woman quite naturally would want him out of the way. Campbell talked to Lowry on the telephone. Lowry told him he had told me everything. Elizabeth Dow was sitting where she could hear Campbell's end of the conversation—enough to know that Lowry had to be disposed of immediately.

"Quite naturally, she wanted to blame the crime on Sue Fisher. Everyone was casting Sue in the role of a crook and it was only natural for the finger of suspicion to point to her.

"So Elizabeth Dow hurried to a pay station, called Lowry and told him to come to Los Angeles at once, to go to a designated spot in Hollywood and wait for her if she wasn't there when he arrived.

"Then the two women really hatched a diabolical plot. They got

Sue to dress in a distinctive costume, to rent a car, put herself in an in-criminating position and then return the car. Then Elizabeth Dow, dressed in that same distinctive costume, picked up her fellow conspir-ator, who was posing as Miss Corning but who was going to have to disappear because Miss Corning's sister was going to arrive. And, of course, her disappearance couldn't look like flight. It *had* to have sinister overtones so that when the body of the real Amelia Corning was discovered that also would reflect back on Sue Fisher.

"As soon as the car Sue had rented was returned, they picked it up, met Lowry at the appointed place, drove him out to the place where they had planned his body was to be found. Remember that Lowry was a loyal employee. He only knew Elizabeth Dow from her voice. He thought she was the head of the subsidiary he'd been working for. He would recognize her voice and follow her instructions to the let-ter."

"Any guess what those instructions were?" Tragg asked.

"Only a guess," Mason said, "But a pretty darn good guess."

"What?"

"Well," Mason said, "Elizabeth Dow probably told him that her companion was Amelia Corning, the owner of the company. That they had decided to destroy some of the books of the company and wanted him to witness the destruction. They said what had been done might have been wrong, so they were going to burn the books and put the money in as income and pay taxes on it."

"That's a guess?" Tragg asked.

"That's a guess," Mason said. "Make your own guess, if you don't like it. Put yourself in Lowry's position. He was in an automobile with the woman he felt was the big boss of the over-all company, and, in addition, the woman who had been giving him instructions which he had been following faithfully all these months. He was going to do whatever they told him to do."

"Which one killed him?" Tragg asked.

Mason shrugged his shoulders and said, "They were both in on it so it doesn't make any difference. In all probability Elizabeth Dow was the one who struck the fatal blow with the letter opener—al-though I have an idea that when you put the pressure on them they'll each try to blame the other and claim the murder came as a sur-prise. However, Elizabeth Dow was the one who had the most to lose because he could recognize her voice. She also was the stronger and more athletic."

Tragg's eyes narrowed. "If that is correct," he said, "and if you surprised the murderers at the job, why didn't they simply toss a match to the gasoline and burn up the evidence?"

"Because they didn't want it burned up," Mason said. "They wanted to make it appear plans had been made to burn up the evidence, but they wanted to be sure the gasoline-soaked body and books tied in with the gallon of gasoline Sue Fisher had bought at the service station.

"The whole thing had to be planned by someone who lived in the neighborhood, who knew the locality, who knew that the branch of the car agency would check out mileage on the rented car when it was returned and then leave it sitting at the back of the lot with the key in the lock. It had to be someone who lived in the neighborhood and it had to be someone who was a close friend of Elizabeth Dow. It's like all those optical illusions—once you see them in their proper perspective you—"

Della Street came pushing forward and caught Mason's eye.

At the expression on her face, the lawyer stopped in mid-sentence.

"Amelia Corning is much, much better," Della Street said. "The doctor has given her a stimulant which has brought her out of it. Her mind is razor-keen. She is asking for you and she's very, very grateful."

Tragg, giving Mason the benefit of his wry, one-sided smile, said, "All right, Counselor, now tell me: How did you manage to get that automobile plastered with fingerprints?"

"That," Mason grinned, "is a trade secret. If Lowry's fingerprints hadn't been on that car I'd have given you a lot to think about . . . and now, if you'll excuse us, we're going to see Amelia Corning. I have an idea I'm laying the foundation for a very substantial fee."

THE END